I0645069

The whole town had been wrong, and now they wanted to apologize, but they were a little too late…

"Misee Sue, Misee Sue!"

John was calling his daughter's name as soon as he went through the kitchen door from the garage. He headed up the backstairs, which would bring him right outside her bedroom door. He just assumed she would be there, hiding herself away in what everyone thought was her shame.

Now, everything would be different.

"Misee Sue," he called again, as he knocked on her bedroom door.

Kia opened her door and stepped out into the hall. She had not gone to the diner with the family and now wondered what was going on. This was very unusual behavior for her dad.

John turned toward Kia.

"Is Misee Sue here?" he asked her.

Kia just shrugged. She didn't want to lie. A shrug could mean anything.

John opened Misee Sue's bedroom door, which was unlocked, of course. He stepped inside the room but stopped short.

The bed was neatly made. The tops of the bedside table, dresser, and chest of drawers were very clean. On top of the dresser, in plain sight in the middle, so that they could not be missed, each with a space between them, were her house key, Clayton's class ring, and the keychain with the keys to the church. There was no mistaking them.

John didn't realize at first that her own car fob was missing. It just didn't dawn on him. Nothing dawned on him, as to the significance of these items.

Kia had come to stand in the doorway.

Then John realized what was wrong. He went to the closet and opened the double-louvered doors to see the empty space inside. He took a step backward. Next, he went to the dresser and pulled out the top drawers.

Empty.

Due to unusual circumstances, when Misee Su makes a "miracle" catch, allowing her high school baseball team to win the state championship, no one sees it. Everyone thinks she's lying—there was no way she could have caught it. The title goes to the other team. Parents, her "soul mate," all the townspeople in this small community totally ignore and shun her, including during graduation. After a week, she cannot stand the hurt and betrayal any longer and drives away to a friend in another town, never to return. Then a farmer comes home from a week-long vacation, raving about the catch he saw Misee Sue make. The championship is overturned, and Misee Sue's team wins the title. Everyone runs to find Misee Sue, now convinced she was telling the truth. But the knowledge is bittersweet. It's too late. She is gone.

KUDOS for *The Catch of Misee Sue*

In *The Catch of Misee Sue* by Mary Jane Bryan, Misee Sue Stone is a high school senior who is playing center field in the championship baseball game when she makes a miraculous catch behind a bush, winning the game. But because it was behind the bush, no one sees it. So no one believes her. They think she is lying in order to win the game, and the other team gets the championship. So the whole town shuns her, even her own family—all except her sister, Kia—as well as her soul mate, whom she plan-ned to marry. Devastated by the hurt and betrayal, Misee Sue drives away and disappears just hours before an eyewitness appears and verifies her catch. Now everyone in town is sorry, especially her family and her boyfriend, but it does them little good, and there is no one they can blame but themselves. But what happened to Misee Sue? Well written with marvelous characters, this one is for fans of romance as well fans of family sagas. A great read. *~ Taylor Jones, The Review Team of Taylor Jones & Regan Murphy*

The Catch of Misee Sue by Mary Jane Bryan is the story of a young woman who is basically honest, but because she makes the normal teenage mistakes, she is not belie-ved at one of the most important times of her life. Misee Sue Stone is eighteen, a senior in high school, a straight-A student, and valedictorian of her high school. She also plays center field on the high school baseball team. In the last game of the year, the playoff for the state championship, Misee Sue makes a miracle catch, winning the game for her school. But because the catch is made behind a bush in centerfield, and because Misee Sue's arch rival says that Misee Sue had said she would do anything to win the game, no one believes she actually made the catch and the umpire awards the game to the other school. Although Misee Sue has never lied about anything important, just little white lies that all of us tell on occasion, her family is humiliated and they shun her, along with her boyfriend, her best friend, and the rest of the town. Hurt and confused, Misee Sue puts up with this for over a week, then she decides to hell with it. She packs up and leaves home. Then a farmer who has been on vacation since the day after the game, but who saw the catch Misee Sue made, comes home and starts talking about what he saw. Now the whole town knows how wrong they were, but Misee Sue is already gone, never to return. With wonderful characters that you can't help but identify with—I am still angry at her hometown—*The Catch of Misee Sue* will stay with you long after you read the last page. Well done for this talented author. ~ *Regan Murphy, The Review Team of Taylor Jones & Regan Murphy*

ACKNOWLEDGMENTS

I would like to thank the excellent, patient, and caring staff at Black Opal Books for their consideration in accepting and producing my "stories." Also, for the artwork on the front cover, so willingly done by my granddaughter, Elizabeth P. Jent

OTHER BOOKS BY
MARY JANE BRYAN
AND
BLACK OPAL BOOKS

No Small Deceit

Errant

Spiral

The Catch of Misee Sue

Mary Jane Bryan

A Black Opal Books Publication

GENRE: FAMILY SAGA/COMING OF AGE

This is a work of fiction. Names, places, characters, and incidents are either the product of the author's imagination or are used fictitiously, and any resemblance to any actual persons, living or dead, businesses, organizations, events or locales is entirely coincidental. All trademarks, service marks, registered trademarks, and registered service marks are the property of their respective owners and are used herein for identification purposes only. The publisher does not have any control over or assume any responsibility for author or third-party websites or their contents.

THE CATCH OF MISEE SUE
Copyright © 2018 by Mary Jane Bryan
Cover Design by Elizabeth P. Jent
All cover art copyright © 2018
All Rights Reserved
Print ISBN: 978-1-644370-05-6

First Publication: SEPTEMBER 2018

All rights reserved under the International and Pan-American Copyright Conventions. No part of this book may be reproduced or transmitted in any form or by any means, electronic or mechanical, including photocopying, recording, or by any information storage and retrieval system, without per-mission in writing from the publisher.

WARNING: The unauthorized reproduction or distribution of this copyrighted work is illegal. Criminal copyright infringement, including infringement without monetary gain, is investigated by the FBI and is punishable by up to 5 years in federal prison and a fine of $250,000. Anyone pirating our ebooks will be prosecuted to the fullest extent of the law and may be liable for each individual download resulting therefrom.

ABOUT THE PRINT VERSION: If you purchased a print version of this book without a cover, you should be aware that the book is stolen property. It was reported as "unsold and destroyed" to the publisher, and neither the author nor the publisher has received any payment for this "stripped book."

IF YOU FIND AN EBOOK OR PRINT VERSION OF THIS BOOK BEING SOLD OR SHARED ILLEGALLY, PLEASE REPORT IT TO: lpn@blackopalbooks.com

Published by Black Opal Books **http://www.blackopalbooks.com**

DEDICATION

*I would like to dedicate this novel to my husband,
Peter M. Bryan, for his patience and
understanding of all my writing projects*

Chapter 1

The ball went high and deep. It seemed to hang in the air forever before starting downward.

Back and around she went, as fast as she could run, which was pretty fast.

She had to run to the back of center field then go around because there was a considerable-sized bush right in the middle of deep center field, about fifteen feet from the out-of-bounds line.

She never took her eye off the ball, even as it disappeared for a split-second behind the bush.

She reached up and over as high as she could. The ball hit against her chest, bounced down into her forearms, which she put together to hold the ball in place, then it rolled down to the edge of her glove, threatening to fall off her hand.

A rapid twist of her wrist brought the ball right inside her glove, but this strange twist of her upper body caused her to lose her balance and fall backward. She fell straight onto her back, landing about one foot from the line.

Although she was short-winded, she held up her glove with the ball in it. Her arm was straight up in the air. She kept it there.

"I caught it! I caught it! I did it! I really did it! We won! We won!"

Chapter 2

Latimer Jones was at the back of his barn, hanging up an old halter, when he heard a loud commotion from the ball field. He knew they were playing today, but this was extra noisy. Something important must be happening.

He stepped out the back door of the barn just in time to see the baseball flying through the hair, seemingly directly toward the bush, up and over it.

At the same instant, he saw Misee Sue running as hard as she could toward it, on this side of the bush, never taking her eyes off the ball. She knew where she was going, of course. He couldn't remember for how many years the kids around here had been playing around this particular bush, so it was second nature for an outfielder to skirt around it in pursuit of the ball.

He saw the ball hit Misee Sue in the chest, bounce around on her forearms, roll down toward the mitt. Then she flicked her wrist and caught it, falling from the twist of her body.

His fist went up in victory.

Good for you, Misee Sue! he thought.

At the same instant, he heard the lowing from his cow at the front of the barn. He turned back inside the barn, closing the door behind him. He locked it and also a second door going into the main area of the barn.

As he walked through the barn to the front, the noise of the ballgame grew fainter and fainter.

But he smiled. He thought, by the sound of things, that Cedarville had obviously won the game with Misee Sue's miraculous catch. At least, that's the way he saw it, a miracle catch. One that would only happen in a lifetime, and that one at the most important time it could. *Kinda like a reverse Murphy's Law*, he thought.

He talked out loud to his cow as he walked through the barn, so that dampened the noise outside even more.

"Now, Bessie, you know I'm sorry. I had to repair the part that broke on the combine. Took some extra tooling. I know, I know, your udder is totally full, and you don't like to be kept waiting. I'm coming, just hold your horses!"

He laughed at his own joke.

As he milked his cow, he thought how important this baseball game was to Cedarville. The town hadn't won a district championship, much less a state championship, ever. And this was what this game was. The state championship game, and against their arch rival, Dover, from two counties over. He thought Dover had won just too many times in the last several years. It was about time someone beat them, and good for Cedarville.

Good for Misee Sue.

Not like back in the day. Latimer played a mean game of baseball back in high school. He thought of games he had forgotten for years. He was the shortstop and a mighty good one until his horse got spooked one day while he was riding and threw him. His knee hit a large rock, split the kneecap, and that knee was never the same again.

There had been talk, by some, about him going on to play ball at college, and then professional ball, but the accident took all that away. Deep down, it was okay with him, though. He really loved the game as a young man, but was not obsessed with playing it enough to want to make it his life's work.

One other young man his age, though, went on to play in the majors for a few years until he twisted an ankle and, like many others, could not play after that. Drove him to drink, it did, and, to this day, he just drank down at the local bar and talked about his "glory days."

Latimer had been sensible enough to stay on the farm, and look what he had now. His wife was gone, but two sons and grandsons came at harvest time to help bale the hay, put it up, and sell a good crop, two times a year. His hay was some of the best around these parts.

So, he understood how Misee Sue must be feeling right now. There were those who would not think he kept up with the ball team, but that was not so. Most home games, he went in just at game time, stood at the end of the bleachers, and watched the game. This was his routine for both football and baseball.

Once upon a time, it was to watch his own sons and their friends, now it was to watch the sons and daughters of the friends of his sons, since his two boys had moved away. But he was genuinely interested in watching the games and kept up with which team won which game and the standings.

He smiled as he thought again of Misee Sue's catch. But his mind went to taking care of this bucket of milk. He had to get his chores finished and get to the house to pack.

His nephew and his wife were coming early in the morning to pick him up. They were going up to Nebraska to visit with his brother and other relatives for a week. He couldn't drive by himself that long a distance anymore, but the nephew and wife were always calling to invite him to go and didn't mind him being along.

He thought that was good, some friends his age seemed to be left out of the younger family plans. He was looking forward to the visit. And he had someone coming by to milk the cow and watch the farm.

Again, he thought, *Good for Misee Sue. She'll be a heroine. The town will probably give a parade in her honor.*

Besides, Misee Sue was a fav of his. Prettiest girl in town and the nicest, too.

Chapter 3

Misee Sue was shouting as loud as she could as the left fielder rounded the side of the bush. All this action had taken place in less than five seconds, just long enough for her to catch the ball behind the bush.

The left fielder was her boyfriend, Clayton. He heard her shouts and saw her flat on her back on the ground at the same time. He stopped short, not sure what he was seeing.

She looked sideways and saw him.

"Clayton, Clayton, I did it! I caught it! Can you believe it?"

She was so excited. She started to rise up, but not before the right fielder and a couple of other players had rounded the other side of the bush.

"No, no, I can't," said Marie, the only other girl player on the team. She was the third baseman. She spoke loudly so everyone gathering could hear.

She was jealous of Misee Sue and always had been, ever since first grade, when she moved to town with her grandparents. Probably, if she had been there for kindergarten, the jealousy would have started then.

"What do you mean, you can't? It was a miracle. I can hardly believe it myself, but *I did it*!" Misee Sue stressed the words. She was jumping around, still with the baseball in her glove. She ran to Clayton and twirled him around.

"You saw it, didn't you, Clayton? You were right there, right at the bush. I can't believe it still!"

She was so ecstatic, knowing that the catch had been the winning catch, that, with this catch, her team had won the state championship for their class, 1-A. For this small town, it would mean the world.

She was so overjoyed that she did not realize that no one else, not even Clayton, was shouting or jumping around, rejoicing with her. She did not realize for several seconds that everyone was just standing there, very still and very quiet, watching her.

She started dancing, twirling around and around. Her cap had fallen off, and one side of her long, blonde hair had escaped its pins. Her hair twirled around her head as she spun. She still had the ball in the glove on her left hand.

Finally, she stopped and looked around. By this time, the other team's players had arrived, as well as the rest of her team, the umpire, and the coaches.

She was surprised. Why weren't they jumping around, excited for the win? "What's wrong?" she asked. "Why aren't you shouting? We won! I caught it! The final out for the other team. We're the state champs!"

But everyone was quiet, still.

What was going on?

"What?" she asked.

A bad feeling hit her in the pit of her stomach.

The umpire spoke first. "Did anyone see the catch?" he asked, as he looked around at the crowd, first to one side of the semi-circle that had formed around Misee Sue, then to the other side.

Several, then more, shook their heads.

"Who was the first to get here? After she said she made the catch, I mean," the man said.

"I was," Clayton responded.

He answered almost reluctantly, Misee Sue thought.

The umpire turned toward him. "Did you witness the catch? Can you vouch for this?"

"Uh…well…no, I didn't. I got here when Misee Sue was on the ground, holding the ball up in the air. She had fallen with it, I guess."

"Yes, I fell after I caught it," Misee Sue said. "My body got off balance with how I had to catch the ball in the glove."

She described, with motions, how the ball hit her chest, and then bounced to her forearms, rolled down them to the edge of her glove, and then she twisted her hand to catch the ball, which threw her left arm to the side, which made her fall.

After she stopped talking, she looked around. No one was smiling. Some were even shaking their heads back and forth, however small.

She didn't understand this. What was happening?

"If no one saw you catch the ball, since it seems like an impossible catch, who's to say you didn't trap the ball on the ground, pick it up, hold it in the air, and say you caught it?" the umpire asked.

Misee Sue's head snapped back like she had been slapped. Her eyes went wide.

"Yeah," Marie interjected, "didn't you just say two days ago at school that you would do almost anything to win this game? To beat Dover and be the state champions for our division, since it hadn't happened for forever? I heard you say that, I'm sure others here did, also. Right?"

Marie looked around. Several nodded their heads up and down, including some players on the team.

"But—but—that was just an expression, one that everyone uses, all the time. I wouldn't lie and say I caught the ball if I didn't. You know that. I don't do things like that. Didn't you hear the 'almost' in that expression? You all know me," she continued, as she gestured around the crowd with her right hand. "I wouldn't do something like that. Yes, I know it seems like an *al-most* impossible catch, but it happened. I caught it!"

She emphasized the almost. She also heard her voice rising to the next level, which showed her stress and dismay.

The umpire gestured as he spoke. "The way that ball was going, there was no way it could have descended straight down like a catch you're describing would allow. No ball, going that fast and high, suddenly plunges downward, just after it clears a bush this tall. The momentum alone would carry it farther back."

"But it did, and I caught it," Misee Sue insisted. But she heard her voice give the slightest hesitation this time. "Here it is, in my glove. Still. Just where I caught it. It never touched the ground. Never."

Suddenly, a player for the Dover team realized the implications of this, what the umpire was going to do. He was going to rule for them, that their two runs to home would provide the win for them.

"We won! We won!" he shouted. He started running around the bush toward the stands, where everyone was still on their feet, waiting for the ruling.

When they saw the player come around the bush shouting, all hell broke loose on the Dover side of the bandstand. People poured out of the stands to greet the other players, who were now running toward home and shouting, jumping around.

The Dover band started playing "Another one Bites

the Dust" then "We are the Champions" by Queen, the old standard go-to victory song for all high school marching bands. In this case, it seemed doubly appropriate.

In the meantime, the umpire was continuing. "In light of the obvious facts of the flight of the ball and the fact that no one but you, Misee Sue, can say that you caught the ball before it hit the ground, I have to rule that Dover wins by one run. Sorry," he said. He turned away.

Misee Sue couldn't believe what she was hearing. She tried one more time. "I caught it, I really did. You know me. I really would not say I did if I didn't, not even to win."

But Marie's words had done their damage, especially with others remembering Misee Sue really had said that two days ago at school.

She couldn't believe her eyes when she looked to Clayton for support. Surely, he believed her. She caught his slight head shake. He mouthed the words, "Sorry, not this time." Clayton was the first one to turn away, push his way through the group that had gathered, leaving her there.

One by one and two by two, the others turned and silently walked away.

There was no joy in Cedarville that day.

If Misee Sue had looked at Marie when Clayton first turned away, she would have seen an evil gleam in her eye and the slightest of smiles on her lips. Marie turned away with the others, not wanting to draw attention to herself.

But Misee Sue's eyes had been on Clayton alone.

Clayton turning away from her.

Clayton not believing her.

Clayton not walking to her side, sticking up for her, saying he, at least, believed her, even if he had not seen the actual catch.

That was the biggest blow of all.

Chapter 4

"Wait!" Misee Sue called. "Wait!"

She stood and watched as, one-by-one, they turned away from her and walked around the bush and out of sight toward the roaring crowd.

For several minutes, she stood where she was, seemingly paralyzed. The ball was still in her glove where she had caught it and showed it to everyone.

The noise of the Dover fans was out of control. She heard their band playing. Yes, their band had come to a baseball game. It was just that important. Cedarville and Dover had been arch rivals for as far back as anyone could remember.

They did it, they really did it. How could they? How could they give the game to Dover when I caught the ball, making the third out for them. That means we won by one run, she thought. *Oh, yeah,* she remembered. *They don't believe me. They might as well have plain-out called me a liar. Well, I guess the umpire did, didn't he?*

The noise seemed to go on forever. It gradually subsided as people started to leave the stands and field.

All of a sudden, the light at center field went out. She looked up and around. The other clusters of lights were still on and would be until the last fan was safely gone. That was how it was always done.

What was Billy doing to her, leaving her in the dark like this? Maybe he didn't know she was still out here.

But, again, all of a sudden, she knew that he knew. He had turned only this light out deliberately because she *was* still here. The others were still on.

Billy? Her friend since kindergarten? It had to be him. He was the one who controlled the lights for every game. But Billy wouldn't believe them. He would know she caught the ball.

Wouldn't he?

A small voice deep inside her said, *No, he thinks you lied.*

She collapsed onto the ground. Her right leg went out in front of her and then bent to the left, drawing her right knee up. Her left leg folded up under her. She was not aware she had fallen. She was numb.

Large teardrops formed in her eyes as she sat there. Slowly, one-by-one, they rolled down her cheeks and fell onto her lap.

She didn't know when she put her ball glove on her right knee and placed her head on it, face down. Her right arm was limp at her side.

The silent tears continued to fall. Silence gave way to soft sobs. When she rose, whenever that would be, it would look as if she had wet her pants. They were already soaked in front from the tears.

This was pay-back with a vengeance. How many times had she sneaked out of the house, gone to a party, then quietly snuck back home? Her parents had confronted her several times for being someplace she was not supposed to be, some place other than where she said she was going to be. The last time, just a month ago, a week before her eighteenth birthday, she was supposed to spend the night at a friend's house, but they both went to the same party. It just so happened that her mom decided to make chocolate chip cookies for the girls, since Misee Sue had skipped dinner that evening. When her mom showed up at the friend's door, she found out the girls had gone to a party, but her friend's mom didn't know where.

The scene with Misee Sue's parents when she finally went home had not been pretty, ending with her dad wagging his finger in front of her face, saying, "This is it. This is the last straw. I give up. The next time you lie about something like this, the next time, I'll…I'll…" He didn't finish what he wanted to say, but his face was filled with fury as he turned away from her.

That resulted in loss of phone privileges, which she just recovered from, and she had to stay home until after graduation. She had just been thankful they had allowed her to play in this ballgame.

A month ago, she had begged off from a date with Clayton, saying she did not feel like going out, but when a friend called a few minutes later to go shopping at the mall in the next town over, she agreed to go. To her, it was not worth it to call Clayton back. He probably had immediately made other plans, also. When he heard about it, however, he was really upset, and asked Misee Sue why she had lied to him. She did not consider it a lie, just a change of plans, but he had not seen it that way.

That must have been why he mouthed the words, "Not this time." She was sure that's what he had said. He meant he was not going to believe her this time.

But what she had done the last two years—the little lie or being where she wasn't supposed to be—had just been normal teenage actions, to her way of thinking. It seemed that everyone did something like that every once in a while. Nothing she did had ever hurt anyone, unless she counted herself, and the "punishment" her dad meted out, which she lived through

No harm had come from her actions.

Until now.

Chapter 5

She had no idea how long she sat there. She must have dozed off because when she finally lifted her head the tears were dry on her cheeks.

Looking around, she saw how dark it was. She looked up at the full sky of twinkling stars and constellations.

The sky was always clear at night at this time of year in this part of the country. She and Clayton often lay back in the bed of his pickup and watched the stars.

They talked nonstop about their dreams and hopes for the future.

About their love for each other. Some people felt that, at eighteen years old, they were too young to know true love, thought that they needed to be "out in the world," sow some wild oats or something, for a while, meet more people, before they committed their lives to each other.

Well, some people in town laughed and said a commitment in high school meant nothing. When they went to college and met other young men, in Misee Sue's case, and other young women, in Clayton's case, that high school "love" would be just that: "puppy love" during high school.

But they both knew for sure they were meant for each other.

They were soul mates. They had been soul mates since third grade—laugh as people might.

Part of those plans was to go to the state university together. They had both received academic scholarships to help with the finances for the families.

It was exciting times, making plans, looking forward to seeing what the world would bring their way.

Now, her world had been shattered. Bad enough was the fact that her fellow team mates looked at her in disbelief. Not disbelief that she had caught the ball with such a miraculous catch, but disbelief that she had lied, they thought, about it, because they couldn't quite believe the catch.

Or, what they thought was a lie, because how could anyone make that catch?

No, it wasn't the fact that the players and everyone had turned away, but the fact that one in particular had.

Clayton!

Her Clay!

How could she forget the look in his eyes? Those beautiful hazel eyes that had looked at her with such love—*had* looked at her with such love.

That last look was full of disbelief and something else she had not been able to put her finger on at the time. But now it came to her.

Loathing!

That was it.

Loathing.

As if she were a snake that he recoiled from. No, more than that, because after the first surprise when encountering a snake, especially a non-poisonous one, he would just laugh and "shoo" it away.

There was no laughter in his eyes the way he had looked at her just now.

Then he was the first to turn away.

The look in his eyes, the disbelief, was too much to bear.

Why hadn't he moved to her, put his arm around her, and said he believed her? Wouldn't *love* itself do that?

More time passed as she just sat there on the ground.

No one came to check on her, not even her mom.

No one cared.

She rose slowly and deliberately. She was stiff from having sat so long in an awkward position. Now, she felt the stiff muscles.

She started walking, with feelings and emotions still

numb. The route home, a shortcut from the ball field, was a familiar one. She didn't have to think about it as she walked along.

She seemed to be sleepwalking, never aware of her surroundings.

From her position in center field, she turned and walked beside Mr. Jones's barn, past his house down his long driveway which would take her to a street on the edge of town.

Duke, Mr. Jones's dog, raised his head from his sleeping position on the front porch. When he saw who it was, by the light from the security light, he lowered his head. He knew and loved Misee Sue. If he wondered, in his dog way, what she was doing crossing the yard this late at night, he felt no threat in it.

Misee Sue had no thought of the dog.

Turning right onto Pine Street, three blocks, then left on Myrtle, brought her three houses down to her own home. These houses were situated on large, spacious lots.

Somehow, she was in her room. She looked around, coming out of her daze.

How did she get here? She didn't remember the walk.

Had Mrs. Johnson's Pit Bull, Max, not barked at her as she went past that house?

That dog barked, day or night, at leaves blowing across the yard. It had never grown used to its environment. If a dog could be a scaredy-cat, he was one.

She silently changed from her uniform to her pajamas and lay down on the bed. She did not have the will or energy to shower. Nor did she want to make a sound to disturb anyone.

Tomorrow would be time enough to talk about everything.

Talk about what just happened.

What *did* just happen?

Chapter 6

Misee Sue slept late. It was past twelve noon when she woke. There were no sounds in the house.

Seeing the time, she quickly jumped out of bed and ran down the back stairs to the kitchen.

Mom would probably have just started lunch. Depending on how many family members were home, it could be anything. But it was always good. Her mom was a natural cook and loved doing it for her family.

No sound came from the kitchen as she descended the stairs. Usually, pots and pans, water rushing through the faucet, or the rattle of plates and silverware would blend with the chatter and laughter of the family.

No one. The kitchen was empty. There were no signs of cooking, or food anywhere.

Something's come up, and they've let me sleep in after all the excitement of last night, she thought. *I'll check the notes.*

The family had a tradition of always leaving notes to show where they were, especially when no one was staying home. She walked immediately to the frig, where various refrigerator magnets held up the notes. They could read "M" for mall, "SM" for supermarket, "De" for Kia's friend, Deanna, and so forth. Each family member knew what the letters meant. The first time something new was used, it was written out then an abbreviation agreed upon later by all the family.

Misee Sue's parents said they began this note system before she was born. They were married for several years before she came and they just continued doing it.

Misee Sue was taught this system and was using it by the time she was in pre-school, although obviously she never went anywhere on her own at that age.

But it developed the habit. Her sister, then brother, after that just naturally did it.

This morning, there were no notes anywhere. No one was anywhere. The house had a preternatural silence about it. When the frig clicked on for its running cycle, she jumped—it was that quiet.

She went to the bulletin board on the wall between the frig and the door to the back stairs. This was another place they left the notes.

Nothing.

There were plenty of the little square notes in the box provided, with assorted pens and pencils standing in a glass beside it, but no written notes anywhere.

Misee Sue was stunned. This had never happened.

Never.

She didn't know what to think about it. She stood for several minutes and then figured it out.

She was being shut out. No one was interested in letting her know where they were. She needed to think about this and what it meant.

As she took a shower and dressed, she thought of the implications of no notes from the family. She checked her phone, which she left in her room before the game last night. There would be a text from someone, probably her mom.

Nothing.

Nothing from family or friends.

She decided just to stay in her room until she heard the family return. She went down the back stairs when she heard her mom's car pull into the garage.

"Mom! Hi! I wondered where you were," she said as she arrived at the bottom of the stairs.

Her mom was coming in the door from the garage, where she always parked her SUV.

"Here, let me help you with those," Misee Sue said.

She reached out with both hands to take some of the plastic bags from her mom. Obviously, her mom had been to the supermarket. Instead of stopping to let Misee

Sue take a couple of the bags as she would ordinarily have done, her mom definitely turned aside and ignored her. She put the bags on the island in the middle of the kitchen.

Misee Sue stood in the same spot, stunned.

Not a word was spoken to her by her mom. Instead, she started putting the groceries in the cabinet.

Misee Sue did not hear her father's car. She turned when he came through the side door.

"Dad—" Misee Sue began. He just held up his hand in an obvious "stop" gesture.

She did.

He ignored her and went to his wife, started to talk to her as he helped put away the groceries.

They obviously ignored Misee Sue.

She stood, still stunned at this action, for several minutes, watching them move from the bags to the cabinet, back to the bags, to the frig, whatever.

Then she turned and silently climbed back up the stairs to her room.

So, that was how it was. She was getting hungry but did not say anything. She did not have time to prepare anything for herself before they had returned. Surely, they would talk to her at dinner.

No.

Her sister and brother had returned by dinner time. They all four were seated at the kitchen table when she came down. No one had let her know to come down.

Usually, her mom would have stood at the bottom of the stairs and called up to her, since her room was right at the top of the stairs.

No place was set for her.

Silently, she went to the kitchen cabinet, got a plate, pulled out a drawer, and took out some silverware. She went to the table to her place, which at least was still empty and had the chair in place.

They had been talking and eating when Misee Sue came down, but now all were quiet. She helped herself to several food items, but nothing was offered to her. She found herself having to reach across for the bowls.

At least they were not denying her any food. She thought they probably just didn't want to be accused of abuse.

Listen to me, she thought. *I sound so bitter.*

Everyone ate in silence. Her brother finished first and asked to be excused by the parents. Her sister followed.

Her mom and dad were almost finished when he asked his wife their plans for the evening.

Misee Sue assumed she was included in this question, as she always had been.

"Why don't we play Pictionary?" she asked. "We've said several times during the week that it's about time for a family game night. Or, is there some other game we would prefer? After I do the dishes, of course, since it's my night for them."

She looked from one to the other, expecting to be answered.

Instead, they stood up at the same time and walked out, leaving her sitting at the table.

They might as well have slapped her in the face, first one then the other. Actually, a slap would not have hurt as much as this. Tears welled up in the corners of her eyes, threatening to fall. She blinked to hold them back.

She was definitely being shunned and ignored.

She did the dishes, taking extra care to leave the kitchen exceptionally clean. She could hear the family laughing as they watched a favorite sit com on TV.

After she finished the dishes, she went up to her room.

She would not call Clayton. When she was in the seventh grade, and just starting to be more interested in him as a young man than just a friend, she decided she would never call him, or run to his car when he honked, at least not for dating purposes. There were always things about school and homework or friends that they called back and forth about.

He would have to respect her enough to call and come to the door to escort her to his car or whatever. She had "stuck to her guns" on this. Clayton always treated her like a lady, forever courteous and respectful.

So, now she would not call him. But she decided to call her best friend. Her best friend's phone went immediately to voice mail, which spoke volumes. Her friend always answered by the second ring, at least. Misee Sue had never left her a voice mail.

Misee Sue's text went unanswered.

She silently cried herself to sleep.

Chapter 7

She was late!

Her mom had let her sleep in, again. But, it was okay. She looked at the clock. She still had time to dress, eat, and go to church with the family.

Her high school graduation ceremony was this afternoon!

What a wonderful time. What an exciting time this was going to be.

Misee Sue was valedictorian, so she had her speech all prepared. She had rehearsed it, changed it, stood, and recited it again and again for each member of the family. Each had patiently and politely listened and commented about how great it was. She had just the right things to say, some personal, some general, a joke at the beginning.

It was the perfect valedictorian speech.

She recited the speech to herself as she showered and dressed this Sunday morning. The dress she wore to church was also the one she would wear under her graduation gown.

She was so engrossed in her thoughts, she did not realize the house was silent again until she started down the stairs to the kitchen.

Was her life going to be from her room to the kitchen by way of the back stairs and back up again?

The smell of bacon and pancakes cooking was missing. They always, *always*, had bacon and pancakes on Sunday morning. It never failed.

Again, the silence.

Again, no one in the kitchen.

Again, no food cooked.

She prepared a bowl of dry cereal for herself. As she ate it, she attempted in vain to hold back the tears.

She had no heart to go to Sunday School or church. She would not have gone to graduation, except for the fact that she was the only one to give a speech.

No one came home after church. She would have to drive her own car to graduation, a car she had received as a graduation present, and the one she would take to college with her.

As a family, they had agreed to have Sunday dinner,

as her special graduation dinner, at a favorite restaurant in the next town over, west of them.

There would be just enough time to get there, eat, and drive back for the three p.m. graduation time.

But she didn't have the heart to go to her special graduation dinner. She wondered if Clayton had shown up with his family and joined her family as planned.

Would they be talking about her?

Chapter 8

She went to the school gymnasium where the graduation ceremony was always held, just in time to line up with the superintendent of schools, the principal, and the salutatorian to march across the stage to their designated chairs. Everyone had practiced this ceremony over and over.

The salutatorian was Marie, who ignored her. Marie's plan was already successfully in place and working far greater than she had anticipated.

When it was time to introduce Misee Sue, you could hear a pin drop in the whole auditorium, it was that still and quiet.

The brief "and, now, here is our valedictorian" was met with silence. Her name was not given. There was no applause.

She bravely started her speech with a joke and her usual bright smile.

Silence.

No smiles from the audience.

She gave her speech, so carefully planned, rehearsed, and praised by the family and her best friend, who was in the graduation group somewhere.

Misee Sue still had not heard from her best friend, and her eyes were so misty she could not make out an individual face anywhere. She made a point of not looking at the spot where Clayton had always been during rehearsals.

⌘

Clayton sat in the middle of the students, a choice he made at the last minute. He didn't want Misee Sue to be able to pick him out very easily.

She rose to silence to give the valedictorian speech.

Starting with her usual beautiful smile, she told a joke. Clayton had to admit it was funny and told in her own particular way. Misee Sue had always been able to tell good jokes that made everyone laugh.

Silence.

She went on with her speech as if nothing was wrong. It was the usual speech, sprinkled with personal accounts of students during the years. All but a few of the students had grown up together, from playing on the playground as toddlers, to now.

When her speech ended, she gave the special class sign, but no one responded. She had accidentally started this special sign back in the ninth grade. It had become a "thing" with this class. No one from another grade used it.

One day, she had tried to do the Vulcan sign that Mr. Spock used on *Star Trek*, which meant "live long and prosper," but her fingers became all entangled with themselves. While a group of friends laughed along with her, the fingers of her right hand went from that sign to the sign for "I love you" in sign language to the "V" for victory or peace. Then she groaned and tried the combination again, and they all three moved in rapid succession. The others in the group tried it, and it worked.

They decided that signaling to each other on occasion, saying, "live long and prosper, because I love you and wish you peace," would become special for the class.

It continued through the last four years. Whenever someone did it, any other classmate who saw it, returned the sign.

Anywhere. Always.

Until today.

ౚౚౚ

The awful silence.

When Misee Sue finished her speech, held up her right arm and gave the sign, no one responded, as the whole class should have.

No one would use it again.

It took her only a split-second to realize the lack of response and the significance of it.

With her head held high, she smiled, that brilliant, happy, special Misee Sue smile. Then she turned and walked away from the podium. She did not return to her chair on the stage. She walked off the stage and continued out of the building. She heard the principal start to say "And, now…" before she was quickly out of hearing.

She would not give them the satisfaction of looking at her after that humiliating lack of response.

איא

She would never know that her name was not called in alphabetical order as each student received his or her diploma. No one ever asked if her name had accidentally been left out or if someone had done it on purpose.

Clayton was secretly glad she had not had to face that. Maybe she had a premonition or something.

She went home to an empty house for the rest of the day.

The special graduation dinner in the next town over went as planned. Clayton and his parents were guests. No mention was made of Misee Sue.

Chapter 9

"Mom?"

"Yes, Clayton?" Mrs. Mathison looked up at her son. She knew what he was thinking. They had not mentioned Misee Sue's name since Friday night, when she had not caught that ball but had said she did. "Now, don't you start talking about Misee Sue," she said. "It's too late for that. If she didn't get any response from that graduation speech of hers today, then it's entirely her own fault. I'm surprised they didn't ask her to step down and let Marie make it."

Clayton frowned at the mention of Marie's name. She had been the first one to speak out against Misee Sue in center field that night. The one with the damning statement about Misee Sue saying she would do anything, stressing the "anything," to win that game, implying that Misee Sue would even lie about catching the ball.

And he had to admit he had come around the bush too late to see the catch.

That damned bush! Why was it still there, anyway? Stupid tradition. The man had died a hundred years ago.

"But, Mom, I really don't believe she lied. I think she caught—"

Clayton didn't have time to finish his thought and sentence before his mom had taken the few steps between them to stand in front of him. She grabbed his arm. "Now, don't be saying that, you hear? You know what your dad and everyone has been saying about the whole losing the game situation and how everyone in town blames Misee Sue. How could she have caught it? You just stay quiet, you hear me? I know how you've thought for years you love that girl, but you're young. A girl who lies like that is certainly not one you would want. Forget her now." Her voice softened. Somewhat. "You must, Clayton, for your own sake. Don't say a word, not to your dad. He's paying for your college, after all. Don't jeopardize that."

Clayton turned away.

His beautiful, wonderful, kind-hearted Misee Sue!

He should have gone to her, supported her, and said he believed her, even though he did not personally see the catch. *Don't you support the one you love?* But for turning away, he now had lost his Misee Sue.

His love! His soul mate!
What was he to do?

Chapter 10

As she climbed the stairs, Misee Sue knew what she was going to do. She had been thinking about it since Sunday, and the decision was made.

The total absence of any acknowledgement of her presence, anywhere in the house, must be what her dad meant when he said, "next time…" Obviously, there was not going to be a next time. He didn't know what to do with what he thought was still another lie, so he—they—were just not doing anything. Period.

In her parents' mind, she had defied and humiliated them one time too many. Being conservative evangelical Christians, as most of the people were in this small town, her behavior at the ball park was just the straw that broke the camel's back. Her dad had had enough.

No one had come to her room all week, so she had no reason to think she would be disturbed this evening. The only one to communicate with her had been her sister, Kia. Kia had sent her a text two nights ago.

~ I believe you caught the ball, but what can I do?

Misee Sue had answered back, *~ Nothing. Don't do or say anything. Do as the family does—you have to live with them, at least for three more years, and then you will be at state and free. And thank you very much for believing in me and believing me! I've seen you glance at me and hoped you didn't think I was lying about that.*

~ Never! Kia typed back. *You would never do that, not to win anything. I'll be quiet, but let me know if I can help you with anything. Love you much.* She put the appropriate emoji on the end.

~ Will do," Misee Sue sent back, *and love you very much, also.*

This was Thursday evening. The seniors had this week off, but there was one more day of school for her brother and sister. They would be gone tomorrow. Her mom and dad would be at work.

She called her grandmother. This was her mom's mother.

Grandma was gone for three weeks to stay with her sister, who had surgery but was having complications. Two other sisters were taking turns staying with her during her recovery, making sure she was at her rehabilitation appointments.

"Hi, Misee Sue, honey," her grandma answered. "How are you, sweetheart?"

Grandma didn't say anything about the game, so maybe she had not heard. She never went to the games because she couldn't sit on the stands or even in a chair that long. The crowds were also too loud, which was just noise in her ears, so she just heard about them later from others.

With worries of her sister, Mae, Grandma probably forgot there had been a championship game. Misee Sue hoped so.

"I'm fine, Grandma. I just wanted to see how you and Aunt Mae were doing."

"Mae's getting a little better, but it's slow going. I'll stay my regular scheduled time and be home next Saturday, as planned. And I'm fine."

"I want you to know I love you, Grandma, and thanks for everything you've done for me through the years. I just realized I've never thanked you enough."

"Well, now, you don't have to do that, sweetheart. You now I'll do anything I can for you, anytime."

"I know," Misee Sue answered. She almost had a catch in her voice. She cleared her throat. "I know," she repeated, "I just wanted to tell you how much I love you."

"And I love you. You will always be my beautiful, sweet Misee Sue, my oldest grandchild."

"I have to go, Grandma. Love you."

"Busy, busy, I know. Bye, love."

They hung up. Misee Sue's eyes misted over. She hoped her grandma wouldn't believe what she heard about the catch.

Misee Sue started organizing her stuff. Clothes, shoes, cosmetics were chosen with care. These were her life now. This was all she would own. After everyone left in the morning, she would take suitcases out of the storage area built in the garage above the overhead door.

She found the disposable phone she used last summer at camp. She had gone for two weeks to camp. She had not wanted to take her expensive smartphone, just in case it was ruined or stolen. So she had purchased this phone with a new number and a certain number of minutes from Walmart on the drive there.

So that she would recognize the number, Misee Sue had always used this phone to call a good friend she met at summer camp last year. They had talked almost every week since then. The phone still had a few minutes on it.

When she arrived at Wichita the next morning, she would call this friend. The friend had invited Misee Sue to come to stay with her anytime.

This was her go-to place. Misee Sue had talked about this new girlfriend some last summer when she returned from camp, but chances were, the family would have forgotten it. She was right. This friend would never be thought of.

Misee Sue's plan went smoothly and efficiently. The

friend was elated that Misee Sue was coming and looked forward to hearing about everything.

In Wichita, Misee Sue went into the main branch of her bank, where a friend of the family worked as the branch manager. Misee Sue withdrew all the money in her savings account and all money from her college fund, which was substantial. She asked for and received it all in cash, telling her friend she was off to college early. Since the manager knew her and her family, no questions were asked.

Fortunately, these accounts were in her name. Her parents said she would learn responsibility at college that way.

She regretted taking the part of the college fund that her grandmother gave her but knew she would understand.

Also, while she was in Wichita, she stopped at a Walmart and put the maximum amount of minutes on the phone that she could, paying with cash. This was now part of her new life.

Her car was not a new one and did not have a GPS or other traceable device on it. That had been a joke with her dad. He made the comment at the time that from now on she would be on her own. He just had to trust her to be in the right places when she should. He had laughed at the time. He didn't know how this would serve Misee Sue so well now.

She would have to store the car somewhere in her

new location, but she would face that after she got to her friend's house. She knew she would be there before she was missed at home.

That thought now caused only indifference. The part of her heart that would, at one time, have cared whether or not she was missed was now stone cold.

∽∾∽∾

She reached her friend's house in the northwest corner of the state around six o'clock that evening. Her car went into one side of a double-car garage with separate overhead doors.

As the door came down, enclosing her car in darkness, her old life ended.

She would become someone else, somehow, someway.

Misee Sue was gone.

Chapter 11

Friday night, after everyone was asleep, Kia crept noiselessly down the carpeted hall to Misee Sue's room.

Fortunately, her bedroom was next door, but that twenty feet seemed to take forever to Kia.

She wanted to talk to her sister. She wanted to reassure her that she believed her, loved her, and see how she could help her with…whatever.

She knew Misee Sue could not go on like this with the family. In fact, she doubted that Misee Sue *would* go on like this.

Kia quietly opened the door, which was unlocked. The layout of the room was familiar to her, but she paused inside the door to let her eyes adjust to the dim light. Misee Sue didn't use a night light, but there was plenty of light through the windows from the tall security light in the backyard.

Kia frowned. There was no lump on the twin bed where Misee Sue should be.

Something was wrong. It was too still, too quiet in the room.

Feeling her way slowly along the edge of the dresser to the nightstand, she turned on the bedside lamp.

She gasped!

No Misee Sue.

Looking around, she saw the closet door was slightly open. She opened it. It was empty.

Kia understood.

Dresser and bureau drawers were empty. Shoes were gone, even though most of Misee Sue's knickknacks and little mementos were still in place. Just a few special books were missing. Kia could tell they were gone, although the remaining books had been re-arranged to fill in any empty spaces.

Way to go, Misee Sue, she thought. *You go, girl! Fly away from this place! Fly so high you touch the sun and never return, which I know you won't. Not with all this. Fly, my beautiful sister. I love you!*

She sent her thoughts to Misee Sue, wherever she was, and felt that Misee Sue heard her.

Kia cried herself to sleep. She knew she might never see her sister again—her beautiful, smart, sweet, kind, big-hearted sister.

She figured Misee Sue had gone that Friday morning when everyone else left the house. That was when Kia, herself, would have gone. Misee Sue was probably long gone by the time Kia went to her room.

Kia vowed to never say a word when it was discovered that Misee Sue was missing. No one would ever know that Kia knew she had been missing from at least that Friday night.

Kia's last thought before she finally drifted off to sleep was, *Yes, fly, fly away.*

Chapter 12

nn's Diner on Main Street was always full for Saturday lunch, from eleven a.m. through two p.m. The townspeople came and went, but the place stayed full during those hours. It was almost a tradition. This Saturday was no exception.

Misee Sue's parents and brother were there. Clayton joined them in a large booth along the front by the window.

Latimer Jones had been gone for a week. His nephew had picked him up early last Saturday morning to drive to Nebraska to visit Latimer's brother, who had fallen and broken a hip. They came back this morning.

As soon as they dropped Latimer off at his house, he set his suitcase inside by the front door, got into his pickup, and came to the diner.

He was as regular as clockwork, but this morning he was later than usual. Because he was late, his favorite stool at the counter was already occupied. It was first come, first served. No one ever expected anyone to move just because they usually sat somewhere.

So today he had to sit at the center of the counter. It wasn't so bad, of course. He knew both the guys on either side of him and greeted them, answered their questions about why he hadn't been there last Saturday. This was just not the end stool next to the rear door, by the door to the kitchen at the end of the counter. Latimer could usually see most of the people from that position.

He had been served his usual meal, the "blue plate special," by Sally, his favorite waitress, when he happened to glance up in the mirror that hung on the wall right in the center of the counter. Funny, he had never really noticed this mirror there before. Was it new? Maybe the owner thought the mirror made it look like there were plenty of people in the diner. That was an old "space" ploy used in retail. Latimer's coffee cup was halfway to his mouth. It landed back on the saucer with a clatter, splashing some coffee over the top. He swirled around on the stool. "John!" he called out.

Three heads went up, including the one belonging to John Stone, Misee Sue's dad. When the other two saw Latimer was looking at him, they went back to eating.

John Stone looked over at him. "Latimer!" he answered, in kind, just not as loud.

"Man, wasn't that a super-duper catch Misee Sue made at the end of the game last Friday night? I'd call it a miracle, I would. Never seen anything like it in my life, and you know I played a mean game of ball, back in the day. You must be super proud of her. Won us the game, didn't it? I could tell by the roar of the crowd. Boy, when she came flying around that bush as fast as she could, I just knew she wasn't going to get to that ball in time, but it seemed to drop down right out of the sky. She was sure dancing a jig with that ball. It hit her in the chest, and then bounced along her forearms."

Latimer chuckled, remembering the sight. He was demonstrating what he was talking about with his own arms. You could always hear Latimer Jones, wherever he was, if he chose to speak at all. He just had one of those voices that seemed to "carry a mile."

He didn't realize, in his excitement of telling about the catch, that the whole diner had become quiet. Not even a spoon or fork scraped against a plate.

The cook had just removed all the food from his grill, so not even that was sizzling as usual. As the expression went, you could have, literally, heard a pin drop.

Latimer continued talking and gesturing. "Then that ball seemed to roll along her glove. I thought for sure it was a goner, but just then, she flicked that glove of hers, and the ball just seemed to fall into it, into the net part." As he talked, he used his left hand to cup it like a baseball glove, with his right hand in a fist like the ball. His right hand, the ball, went into the net of the glove, which was his left hand. "That gal just clamped her glove around that ball and didn't let go. I knew she was gonna fall down, of course, the way she had to dance and twist around to catch that ball. I just knew her feet were going to get tangled up. Sure enough, she fell straight backward. Had to hurt like h—like everything, pardon, ladies—when she hit like that, but she held that ball up in the air the whole time." His left hand, with the imaginary glove on it, holding the imaginary ball, went up in the air, his arm extended all the way up. "Like I said, it was a miracle catch, once in a lifetime, if even then. Never seen anything like it, no sirree," he repeated. "I heard her call, 'I did it, I did it, I caught it!'"

John Stone had stood up about halfway through Latimer's spiel. His mouth was hanging open. He was looking at Latimer like he was from outer space, or something. John found his voice. "Latimer, are you telling me that you saw Misee Sue catch that ball?"

"Of course, I saw it. Ain't that what I been telling you all? That gal's something else, always has been." Just then he noticed how still and quiet the diner was. He looked around. "Hey, what's going on?" he asked.

"Would you be willing to swear that Misee Sue caught that ball, like you just said, in a court of law?" John asked.

Latimer frowned. "Of course, I would, on a stack of Bibles, if need be. What's going on?" he repeated.

Clayton had also jumped up. "You all know what this means, don't you?" He looked around the diner. "We *won* that game!"

"Of course, we won that game, thanks to that super catch of Misee Sue's," Latimer said again. He wondered if everyone here had suddenly gone deaf. "Who says we didn't?" he asked.

"Where's Coach?" Clayton asked. He looked around the diner, to the spot where Coach and his wife usually had lunch, just about this time of day.

Someone across the room spoke up. "Grace and him went to their cabin this weekend to fish and get a little R and R. Left yesterday. I ran into him at the hardware store on Thursday, and he told me then."

The cabin was on Cowley Lake, over by Arkansas City.

"Then let's go get him," Clayton urged. "Who's coming?"

He was already heading toward the door. John Stone was right behind him.

Several men called out, to wait for them, they were coming. They either left money on their tables to pay for the meals or simply left it up to the wives or other friends to pay.

Sally would have carried them, anyway. This was just that important.

Latimer felt a hand touch his arm and he turned back to the counter. Sally had touched him.

"What is it?" he asked her.

"Just finish your meal. I'll tell you all about it."

As he picked up his fork, Sally told him about the catch of Misee Sue that no one else saw, and no one then believed she caught it, that she had picked it up off the ground and lied about it, allowing the umpire to declare Dover the winner.

Latimer stopped her there. He was appalled. "But I saw it. I'm not nobody. That was a great catch."

The few remaining customers, mostly the wives, heard the rest of the story. It would be repeated, surprisingly accurately, for many, many years to come.

"After she fell and was holding that ball in the air, yelling how she caught it, I saw young Clayton come around the bush. Bessie mooed just then, calling me. I knew her bag must be really full, 'cause I had to repair a part on the combine and ran into complications. Since Misee Sue caught it, and Clayton was there, I knew everything was okay. I stepped back into the barn, you know where that back door on the barn is..."

Heads nodded.

"...and I went to the front to milk Bessie. With the door between me and the back of the barn by then, and in Bessie's stall, I couldn't hear anything else, except a drum beat. I figured we were celebrating big time. I went to process the milk, left Willie a message to come and get it on Saturday morning, then packed for my trip. I went to bed early since Carl was picking me up at five a.m. Takes all day to get to Omaha, you know, and my brother's place is about thirty miles beyond that. I can't believe, though, that no one believed that gal. Never known her to be dishonest in her life. Right friendly, and helpful, too. Remember that summer she came to help with the baling? Strong as an ox. Made everyone there think they were happy to be working in that hot sun! Not believe her? I've never heard of such a thing!"

"Want your usual blackberry cobbler, Latimer?" Sally asked.

"You know, I think I'll take a piece of the cherry pie today. I know Ethel makes them for you, and she's a mighty fine pie maker."

When Sally placed the pie in front of Latimer, she said, "Your meal is on the house, today, Latimer. Enjoy your pie."

"Why, thank you, Sally, that's mighty kind of you. I need to be gone more often!"

They laughed.

He would only understand later how important he had just become to the town.

Wives paid up and then quietly left.

There were phone calls to make.

Chapter 13

Misee Sue sat with her friend, Gail, and Gail's mother, Barbara, on their covered patio, sipping sweet tea. It was just right, and Misee Sue told Barbara so.

"I've used the same brand of tea, same amount, same amount of sugar that my mother used for years and years. I figured, why mess with a good thing, right?"

Gail and Barbara had heard Misee Sue's story. They were surprised that Misee Sue was not bitter about the whole situation. Barbara suspected that the hurt was so deep, Misee Sue was still numb. At a later date, it would all set in.

"I just wish I could become someone else, take another name, whatever. I've thought and thought, though, and I just don't see how I can do that. Sure, I can hide the car forever, somewhere, I know, but then there's me. I'm the important 'thing' to hide."

A sudden idea hit Barbara. She would not be able to explain later where it came from. She had not thought about it for many years. "Stay right here, don't go away. I have an idea. Wait for it."

Misee Sue and Gail looked at each other, raising their eyebrows.

"Where would we go?" they asked, but Barbara was already through the French doors.

"I wonder what that's all about?" Gail asked. "Mom seemed pretty excited. Oh, well, we'll find out soon enough."

It was about fifteen minutes before Barbara returned. She had two folded pieces of paper in her hand.

"Sorry it took so long. I thought these were in one place, but I guess I moved them to another place some-time through the years." She sat down and then held out the papers toward them. "This is something I have not thought about for a long time, but now seems the perfect time for it to be used for something." She looked at Gail. "I'm about to tell you something that very few people know, certainly not you. Your dad knows, because I thought it only fair to tell him when we started dating. I thought we had something special the minute I met him but knew if he didn't accept this—" She held up the two folded pieces of paper, again. "—then there was no rea-son to continue our relationship. This was when we started dating, of course. I had to see his reaction. Fortunately, he never hesitated nor wavered for a split-second when I told him. He immediately took me in his arms and held me as I cried. I knew in that moment that he was the love of my life, my soul mate."

Gail and Misee Sue became "curiouser and curiouser" as Barbara talked.

"This is a birth certificate, Gail, of a child I had when I was only sixteen."

Gail was appropriately shocked. "Mom!" she cried. Then she was speechless.

"I know, I know. It's a shock, and I hope you will forgive me when you hear the story. This is a birth certificate, and this other piece of paper is a death certificate. My baby lived only one day. It was full-term, but there were heart defects, so she lived only that little while. And she was a pretty little girl. I never, for one moment, considered aborting the baby. This was a little life who didn't ask to come into the world. She was on the way because of my bad choices. I was determined she was not going to be punished for my mistakes. I felt aborting the fetus would be a bigger mistake.

"The young man never knew I was pregnant. Fortunately, my dad took another job in another state just at the time I was three months along, so we moved. No one in my hometown, this town, knew about it. I stayed inside for the remainder of my pregnancy, going to the doctor when necessary. I've never reconciled the fact whether it was fortunate or unfortunate that the baby died in the hospital. We had a story ready, about the child being that of a cousin who was irresponsible, on drugs, and that we agreed to take the baby. No one would have questioned it. Probably our friends at that time would have praised us for being willing to raise the child. But that became a moot point, of course."

She looked sad for a few seconds. This had brought up a sad memory. She also looked at Gail. She needed her approval.

Gail put her hand on hers. "I'm sorry for your loss, Mom, you were so young. But it's okay, especially since Dad knows."

Gail seemed to forget that she was only eighteen now, herself.

Immediately, Barbara brightened. "That was long ago, though, but it gave me a wonderful idea as we talked, for Misee Sue. Look at the name and date on the certificate."

Gail and Misee Sue took it and looked at it together.

"Elizabeth Ann Conners," they read out loud, together. Gail looked up. "Conners is your maiden name, Mom."

"Yes, the only last name I had to give my baby. And social security numbers were not mandatory back then for babies under one year old, so there is no record of her that way."

They were reading the birth date.

"March 11, 1993."

"Aren't you eighteen, Misee Sue? Otherwise, you couldn't legally be here. You probably would already have an Amber Alert out for you, or something. If you're eighteen, this is only one year before you were born. Would you like to become Elizabeth Ann Conners? We buried her quietly in a small, country cemetery with only five of our family members there. Two of them have passed on. I know someone who could make this happen." Barbara looked at her daughter. "Don't you know who I mean?" she asked Gail.

"Uncle Nelson!" Gail cried. "Of course, he could make it happen. Personally, I mean. What an idea, Mom!"

Uncle Nelson held the contract on a state tag agency in the next town over, a much larger town than this, about twenty miles away. Using this birth certificate, he could issue Misee Sue a driver's license in this name.

"But you really wouldn't mind if Misee Sue uses your child's name, that she becomes Elizabeth Ann Conners?"

"No, not at all. In fact, I think it's perfect."

When Misee Sue heard Barbara's plan, it did seem perfect. It all depended on four or five people keeping it secret, which she was assured of.

"In fact," Barbara said, "Nelson, my uncle, and Gail's great-uncle, was one of the people who knew about my baby and attended the burial for her. He has never spoken of it, to me or anyone else. Families keep secrets, you know, just as they should. You never know how many skeletons are in any given closet!"

They laughed.

"Also," Barbara remarked, "now I see a greater plan because of my baby. The universe moves in its own special way."

There was a somber moment, which Barbara herself broke.

They talked over the plan. It all rested on Uncle Nelson's cooperation. Barbara called him as they sat there. She told him all about Misee Sue. He wanted to meet her, in person but said it sounded like it would work. It was outside the law, of course, but it could just work.

They agreed on a time to be at Nelson's that evening. In fact, he invited them all to dinner. He said his wife wouldn't mind, and they didn't get together often enough, anyway.

The rest of the conversation with the ladies was very exciting. They discussed what Misee Sue could be called. They agreed it wouldn't be Elizabeth, so it would be less traceable. They thought of "Liz," "Betty," "Eliza," and a couple of others, but finally agreed that Misee Sue looked like a "Beth." Misee Sue liked it, also, so from that moment on, they called her Beth.

That afternoon, they walked to the local pharmacy to buy a pair of clear-lens glasses and a package of hair color. They cut and dyed Misee Sue's hair.

All went well at the family dinner. Nelson and his wife liked Beth on sight. This was the Beth with the glasses and short, dyed, dark-brown hair. This is the way they would always see her.

Chapter 14

Coach Smith and his wife, Grace, had been out early on Lake Cowley with their bass boat. They were unsuccessful at catching any bass, after trying a few spots known for having fish in them. They were now off shore from the cabin. They could still see the cabin in the distance. All their lines were in the water. They were in waiting mode.

Coach looked up when he heard a truck motor from the direction of their cabin. When three vehicles came into sight and pulled in a row at his cabin, facing the lake, he had a feeling in the pit of his stomach that something important was up.

He looked through his binoculars to see Clayton's truck. John Stone was getting out the passenger side.

What was going on?

"What is it?" Grace asked. She had noted the trucks herself. She had her hand over her eyes, trying to make out what was happening.

"I don't know, but it must be something important. I see Clayton and John Stone. Also, Kaden and Jack, others."

Just then his cell phone rang. He answered it. It was John Stone.

"Coach, we see you out on the lake. Can you come in, right away? There's something very, very important you need to hear about."

"What is it?" Coach asked.

"Just come on in, okay? It's not something for a phone."

"Sure, just give us a few minutes to get our lines out of the water and get there."

It was a good fifteen minutes before the boat made it to the dock. Two of the men were there, took the lines Coach threw to them, and tied up the boat.

Coach helped his wife off the boat and then turned to the others. "Okay, what's so important you took us from our fishing? Come on up to the deck." He wasn't upset, though. It had been a miserable day for fishing. In fact, he was just about to suggest to his wife that they come on in when the vehicles appeared. "Maybe we can talk Grace into getting us something to drink." He smiled at this wife, who graciously consented.

She left them to walk up the incline to the cabin.

Looking around, to make sure the boat was secure, they started walking up the hill.

Comments of "you're not going to believe this," and "guess what?" came from the men.

They settled on the porch, with beer for the men and Grace's homemade lemonade for Clayton. When Coach heard what Latimer had told them, he was truly shocked.

He sat for a few moments, speechless.

"What can we do?" Clayton asked. "Surely there is something that can be done."

Coach found his voice. "First, we need to make an appointment with the state commissioner. I know him personally. We went to university together, had the same major. Then he just chose to go another route with his degree, and he's done well. I just saw my mission in life as coaching high school sports in a small town, and that dream is here. It's too late today to call him, and—"

Clayton shook his head. "I don't think so. Sorry to interrupt you, Coach, but I think he will see this as something worth disturbing him for. If he's out on a lake, like you were, surely he would come in for this, after you explain everything to him."

"Maybe you're right. He might see it that way," Coach responded.

He took out his cell phone. The commissioner's number was on speed dial. The commissioner answered right away. After their greeting, Coach got right down to the point, explaining what he had heard, the whole situation.

The commissioner was amazed. "I don't think there is a precedent for this. I can't recall it ever happening in this state, maybe not in any state. Let me think about and research this and get back to you, okay? I'll get on it right away. I won't forget, but it might take through Monday, when some others are back in their offices. It may be that Mr. Jones will have to come in, sign a sworn affidavit, and all that. Just don't turn off your phone, okay?"

Coach knew his friend was teasing. "No way, don't worry about that," he said. They hung up. He turned to the others. "Now, it's just wait and see. That gives us the next couple of days to be on pins and needles. The commissioner will call Monday morning, probably to set up a meeting to talk to Latimer and hear in person his eye-witness account of The Catch."

It was funny. The people had already been referring to the catch as "The Catch," with capital letters. You could hear it in their voices.

The men headed back to their town. They wanted to talk to Misee Sue as soon as possible, tell her about Latimer Jones and what Coach was doing. Big-time apologies were in order, they thought. They each thought the whole thing would blow over with her. She would understand their way of thinking at the time.

They were in for a surprise, of course.

Coach and Grace stayed on at the cabin but decided

the fishing was no good. They just relaxed, talked about this new development. Grace hoped the win would be overturned. She had never made a comment about Misee Sue, but secretly she felt the girl *had* caught that ball. Now, they found out she really had.

Good for her!

Chapter 15

isee Sue, Misee Sue!"

John was calling his daughter's name as soon as he went through the kitchen door from the garage. He headed up the backstairs, which would bring him right outside her bedroom door. He just assumed she would be there, hiding herself away in what everyone thought was her shame.

Now, everything would be different.

"Misee Sue," he called again, as he knocked on her bedroom door.

Kia opened her door and stepped out into the hall. She had not gone to the diner with the family and now wondered what was going on. This was very unusual behavior for her dad.

John turned toward Kia.

"Is Misee Sue here?" he asked her.

Kia just shrugged. She didn't want to lie. A shrug could mean anything.

John opened Misee Sue's bedroom door, which was unlocked, of course. He stepped inside the room but stopped short.

The bed was neatly made. The tops of the bedside table, dresser, and chest of drawers were very clean. On top of the dresser—in plain sight in the middle, so that they could not be missed, each with a space between them—were her house key, Clayton's class ring, and the keychain with the keys to the church. There was no mistaking them.

John didn't realize at first that her own car fob was missing. It just didn't dawn on him. Nothing dawned on him as to the significance of these items.

Kia had come to stand in the doorway.

Then John realized what was wrong. He went to the closet and opened the double-louvered doors to see the empty space inside. He took a step backward. Next, he went to the dresser and pulled out the top drawers.

Empty.

Another step backward. He looked up a Kia.

"She's gone," he said, incredulously.

His expression told her he couldn't believe that Misee Sue was not here, sulking in her bed, as the family intended.

"It looks like it," Kia answered. Still, no lie. A non-committal comment.

She stepped back into the hall as John stormed past her to the stand at the top of the stairs.

"Doris, Doris, come here, quick!" he called to his wife.

She had been puttering around in the kitchen, putting groceries away.

At the tone of his voice, the anxiety she noted, she lost no time in running up the stairs. She imagined all sorts of things that might have happened to Misee Sue.

John led her to Misee Sue's bedroom door.

"Look everywhere. No clothes, no makeup, nothing. She left her keys and Clayton's class ring on top of the dresser so we couldn't miss them. She's gone. Misee Sue is gone!"

Well, what did you expect? Kia thought. *Don't you dare blame Misee Sue.*

Doris's right hand went to her heart. It was pounding. "When did this happen? How could this have happened?" *Just because we were disciplining—okay,* she admitted to herself, *punishing—Misee Sue for what we thought was a big-time lie just to win the game, has she run away from home?* "Oh, no. She's gone, run away after all this ball business. We need to call the police," she said. "Misee Sue has run way from home. We need to report this."

"Doris," John said, seriously. "Misee Sue is eighteen years old. I don't think they would call it running away from home, especially since it's obvious she intentionally packed and took all her personal items. They would say she could make her own decisions at this age. We have no authority to make her come home."

"What about her car? Can't we track her because of that? We bought that, it's ours."

"Remember, we put it only in Misee Sue's name, so she would have the responsibility for it. It's hers, not ours. It was her graduation gift from us, so she would have a good car at college. The insurance is in her name only."

"But it has a tracking device, doesn't it? That's what I meant. We can locate her with that."

"No, it doesn't. But, okay, I'll call Donald, see what he can do at this point." He looked at Kia. "Did she tell you anything about this?"

"No, nothing," Kia said. Again, not a lie. Boy, was she glad her dad had worded the question that way and she could answer truthfully. If he had asked if she knew anything about Misee Sue being gone, she would have had to lie.

Her parents turned to go downstairs.

"Let's make sure she took her car."

Kia breathed a sigh of relief and went back into her room. With any luck, they would not ask her any more questions. They didn't.

Chapter 16

"How long has she been away from home?" asked Donald, the chief of police.

It was Saturday night, but he took calls at home. Usually, there weren't that many of them.

"I told you, we really don't know, for sure," John replied. "When we got back from the lake after talking with Coach, I went up to tell her what Latimer said. Her room was empty. Her clothes and shoes are gone, most of her personal items. And her car, of course. We have to report that."

John felt Donald's hesitation on the other end of the line.

"Um…don't I remember you guys celebrating Misee Sue's eighteenth birthday in March? I was invited, just couldn't make it. That was her eighteenth, wasn't it?"

"Yes," John replied.

He was afraid he knew what Donald was going to say. At eighteen, Misee Sue was no longer a minor, and her parents did not have the authority to make her come back home, wherever she might be. And the car *was* in her name.

"And didn't I hear you say at the time that you guys put the car and insurance in Misee Sue's name only, for her to pay her own insurance, to teach her some responsibility as she went away to college?"

"Yes," John said, again, but not as firmly.

"Have you entertained the possibility that Misee Sue has simply moved out of the family home, wants to live on her own somewhere. She's legal in doing that. I hate to have to say that to you, but it's the law. There is nothing in Misee Sue's actions that I could go after her for, nothing to make her come back to your home. And, frankly, what with her packing all her things like that, leaving the house keys and Clayton's ring, it sounds like that's what she wanted to do, and she did it."

Personally, to himself, Donald was glad for Misee Sue. Yes, he had been one of the ones who shunned her, but he thought the parents were just disciplining her for what they thought was her lie, and that, after a time, they would relent, and she would have learned her lesson. He never dreamed that she would have let the whole matter affect her so deeply. At least not to the point of leaving home. But, knowing human nature, there was no accounting for how any given person would react to the same situation.

And he had to admit, the whole town did a pretty good job of shunning her, shutting her out. How would Misee Sue know that it would end soon?

And just how well did he know John and Doris Stone? Was it really simply discipline or done maliciously because they were mad at their daughter? Had they done this before to Misee Sue or Kia?

"Can't you put an APB or something out on the car?" John asked. "Publish the license number, make, and model, at least to the various law enforcement agencies, if you can't make it to the public? You can't miss a car like that, with that color."

Surely, he thought, *there was something the police could do.*

"Whichever agency might agree to announce it, would only be doing it as a courtesy—fellow agency to fellow agency, that sort of thing. They could not legally require their officers to search for this vehicle, since no crime has been committed and, again, the fact that Misee Sue is eighteen. If they saw it, and the license matched, they could only report it, not stop the vehicle if the driver wasn't doing anything illegal. Sounds like you might just have to wait until Misee Sue decides to come home, and she probably will, when she runs out of money. How much money would you say she has on her?"

"Oh, my gosh!" John exclaimed. "You just made me

think of something I hadn't yet thought of, I hadn't gotten that far in this whole situation."

"About the money?" Donald asked.

"Yes. Her bank accounts are in her name only. We did that, along with the deal about the car and insurance, so she would be responsible for her own college spending. We told her if she ran out, then she just ran out. She had enough in her accounts to cover expenses for at least two years of college, maybe more."

"Then I doubt if any bank will tell you anything about them. Did she have multiple accounts in her name?" the chief asked.

"Just two. She had a personal one and one earmarked for college, a fund that we did not have to pay taxes on the interest for the last four years. No penalty for withdrawal, that sort of thing."

"If she's thought of all that money, and she probably has, since it sounds like she planned her 'get-away' very well, then she's withdrawn all of it. The bank won't even tell you if she's been there, or anything. Those privacy laws, you know. You probably get a copy of them in the mail every once in a while, and I bet you never bother to read it, do you?"

"No," John agreed. "But this is not about me—us. It's about Misee Sue. What would she know?"

Donald laughed. "Oh, just about a thousand percent more than you would ever suspect she does. The young people these days are pretty savvy about things, especially things pertaining to the law, whether they ever plan to break it, or not."

Even this little town had its percentage of teens who seemed to know everything.

ⅇⱷⱸⱷ

Several people called in the next few days, saying they had spotted the car. Each sighting was checked out. It was always the correct car, even color, but each caller had to admit that they did not get the license number before they called it in. They were all dead ends.

Clayton came up with another plan. They all knew Misee Sue had talked for years about going to the state university.

They contacted the campus police, who agreed that when the first day of matriculation came, they would be posted all over the campus to spot Misee Sue. Everyone would have a photo.

The other alternative was not to be thought about—that Misee Sue, having driven away, had been accosted or attacked at some point, and her body was in a shallow grave somewhere or just thrown out in the deep woods or down a ravine, somewhere no one ever went.

That thought went through each mind, but was not voiced, except by the chief, who felt it was his duty to cover all angles. "If she's the victim of foul play, then the car has probably already been sent through a chop shop and is now 'parts is parts,' so to speak. In that case, it will never be located."

Although everyone silently agreed with that assessment, they refused to talk about that possibility for the rest of the summer. They just knew Misee Sue wouldn't miss her college registration and would show up then.

Chapter 17

Beth went to church with Gail on Sunday. If she were going to live in this town, she might as well start being seen and meet people.

One of Gail's friends, Brian, wanted to know what was going on when the three of them walked to the parking lot together.

"Why don't we come out to your place for lunch and we'll tell you," Gail said. She invited them, but she was that good of friends with Brian that she could do that.

"Great idea," he agreed. "You know Sam always leaves me something to eat, and that's always too much. She declares I'm too skinny and need some meat on my bones!"

They laughed.

He explained to Beth that Sam was really Samantha,

a middle-aged lady who came to his house three times a week to clean the house and cook for him. She always cooked enough for the other days, putting items in the frig and freezer for him to heat up or put in the microwave.

Brian had a farm three miles out of town. His parents had been killed in a car accident three years before, so that left the place to him, their only child. He had seriously considered selling the place but just couldn't bring himself to do it. He had a college degree, and luckily he got that in horticulture science.

Maybe he knew that he would end up running the farm at some point. If asked, he would have told everyone it would be when his dad passed in his old age. His responsibilities just came sooner than he planned, that's all.

They were halfway through their salads and through Beth's story, when Gail put down her fork suddenly. She almost choked on her salad, having a mouthful at the time. That's what Beth and Brian thought was happening.

Brian jumped up, ready to do whatever he could.

Gail had swallowed. "Sit, sit," she said. "I'm sorry I scared you. I'm not choking or anything. I just had a thought that I think is so brilliant, it amazes me."

Beth and Brian looked amused. This had better be good, scaring them like that.

Gail looked at Brian. She started pointing toward his big barn with her index finger, wiggling it back and forth, like Blake Shelton did toward himself on *The Voice*. "Is that garage space still empty beside the main part of your barn?" she asked.

"Of course, of course, I see what you're getting at. I'm surprised I didn't think of it myself. Just been hit with a dumb stick today, I guess."

Beth was looking back and forth between them. Her confusion showed on her face.

"You want to hide your car, right?" Brian asked.

"Oh, definitely, as soon as possible and as far out of sight as possible," she answered.

"Then we'll show you something right after lunch. It can wait, and this lunch is too good to interrupt," Brian said.

They had a leisurely lunch, ending with coffee on the back porch, which had plenty of shade from beautiful, big trees. A nice breeze was blowing. But to help with cool down on any given day, the family had installed three large ceiling fans across the porch. Brian turned them on to help generate a refreshing breeze.

At last, he put down his coffee cup. "Okay, since Beth is probably 'chomping at the bit' to hear our great news, let's show her."

They walked to the large barn, and it was indeed large. Built in the old-fashioned way, it went up three stories, with the traditional door in the front on the third story to haul bales of hay up and store them in that top story. Brian explained that he still used it. Not only did he have about a hundred head of cattle, but baled many acres of hay. Some of the hay was to feed the cows during the winter, but he also sold some.

When they came even with the large, open doors, he said, "wait here a moment."

Gail had a smile on her face.

Brian was back in a minute. It didn't look like he had anything in his hand, so Beth really wondered what was happening.

They walked next to the big barn area, to a smaller double-door, but still a part of the barn. It had been built as part of the whole original barn.

Brian brought out a key and opened the large padlock that kept the doors shut.

Gail took one handle of one of the doors and Brian took the other. Both walked backward and opened this area. It looked like a large garage, with plenty of room for a large tractor, which was its original purpose. It was now empty.

She hoped it was for her car, to hide it until they could think of something.

To her relief and joy, it was for her car, but Brian offered it to her on a permanent basis, for the car to be stored there indefinitely.

"I don't use this garage for anything. I built another large shed that holds several tractors and the combine, so I could have them all in the same area. It's around the back of this old barn, and more convenient to get the equipment out of and heading into the fields. This is your space, if you want it. And I even have a large covering, if you want it. It's a spare, also."

Beth couldn't believe what she heard. It brought tears to her eyes. She reached up to wipe them away.

Brian grinned. "Well, it's not that bad. You don't have to cry about it."

"It's not bad at all, it's super. It's more than I ever hoped to find, and the offer to leave it here indefinitely is just what I need." Beth looked at Gail. "I didn't want to go to that summer camp, I really didn't, but now I know why I did. Not only did I meet you, an instant best friend at the time, but now for all this." She waved her hand, stopped at Brian, and smiled. "You're going to be my second best friend, I know it."

"What do you mean, 'going to be'?" he asked. "We are already. I'll just have to work hard to replace Gail as first best friend."

They all laughed

But she had known it, that's the strange thing. The very instant they met at the church, she felt an instant rapport with him. Something just clicked between them.

Brian was five years older than she and Gail, just the right age for an older brother, a special friend.

The two ladies drove right into town and brought Beth's car back to the farm.

Brian gave a whistle when he saw it.

"Wow! You have a Chevrolet Camaro SS Turbo.

What is it, around a 2009, 2010? And the classic Canary Yellow. It's too bad you want to park this thing, but I understand, of course."

"Yes, a 2010, and you must know your cars," Beth responded.

"I know these cars. I've been a shade-tree mechanic since I was an early teen. Dad and I always did our own repairs, restored a couple of classics to sell them. We made a good profit on them, but most important of all, we just enjoyed doing it. I worked for Dale a lot during the summers."

Dale owned the local auto body repair shop.

Brian looked at Gail, who nodded. She remembered him working there.

"No, the most important thing of all was the fact that you and your dad worked on them *together*," Beth said.

"You're right, of course, especially since…" He didn't finish.

"Sorry, I didn't mean to bring up a sad memory," Beth said.

"You didn't, I have those great memories," Brian said. "You two help me put the tarp on this."

As they worked, he asked permission to drive it around the farm at least once a week, just to keep it running in tip-top shape. It was not good for a vehicle to just sit. Beth said of course he could. It would remain licensed for almost a year. She had just received it as a graduation gift the first part of May. This was the last of May.

They shut the double doors. Brian handed Beth one of the keys to the padlock he used to secure the garage.

"Let me show you where I'll hang the spare key, in case you ever need it, and I'll use to drive the car some."

Inside the left of the large barn doors, there was a line of hooks. There were various keys and other items hanging from them.

"Fourth hook from the left will be yours," he said, as he put the key there, hanging from a string.

"And these are yours," Beth said. She held up the car fobs. He held out his right hand, and she let them drop into his palm.

Out of her life. She had not had the car long enough to really be attached to it.

"You have to name her, you know, I didn't yet. Just couldn't think of the right name."

Brian laughed. "I knew it, I just knew it. You name your cars. I do, too, I knew we had that in common. But why do you think it's a 'she?'" he asked.

Beth shrugged. "Don't know. If it seems like the opposite to you, then go for it. I don't care anymore."

Brian and Gail both knew she could have said that with bitterness, but she didn't. It was just a statement of fact. That car just was not part of her life now.

It would never be again.

Brian invited Beth to come back, anytime.

"Only if you will let me ride one of those beautiful horses I saw in the paddock behind the barn," she said.

She grinned at Brian.

"Oh, you ride? Really?" he asked. He was excited.

"Does she ever! She's an excellent rider. There were a few horses at the camp for whoever wanted to schedule them and take a ride," Gail added.

"That's wonderful, and, of course, you can ride one, or all of them, depending on which one wants to be ridden by you that day. What about tomorrow morning? I usually go about nine every morning," Brian said.

"I think we have some business to attend to tomorrow, but I'll be here Tuesday morning. Oh, no, I forgot I don't have a car to get here. Don't we get so used to having our cars that we just don't think about it?"

"That's okay," Gail said, "you can drop me off at work each morning, then come out here. I just walk to lunch each day, anyway, and sometimes take my lunch and eat in our employee lounge."

"Thanks so much," Beth replied. "You're doing so much for me." She turned to Brian. "And you, also, Brian, of course, just letting me store the car here until we figure this all out. I also want to check each day at businesses here in town. I know there's not a lot of choice, and maybe nothing available, but I would like to put in applications, to the ones that will allow me to, for further reference. Maybe one of them will remember me when someone quits."

"What type of work are you looking for?" Brian asked.

"I'm not particular at all. I would just like to be able to support myself and make a little money."

"So, you think you want to stay here? Aren't we too little for you? There are certainly more opportunities in a bigger city."

"No," Beth answered. "This town is just the right size for me. Besides, I don't think anyone will be looking for me in a place like this. I think they will check the big cities."

"You may be right," Brian returned. "I'll certainly keep my ears open for anything that might come up. Sometimes the locals don't put a job opening in the paper, it just goes around town by word of mouth. Anyone interested shows up at the place and talks to the owner. Come out to ride after your job hunting is done. The horses aren't going anywhere!"

Chapter 18

First thing Monday morning, Beth went to the social security branch office in a neighboring town, the county seat. Using the original birth certificate that Barbara supplied, she was able to get a social security number.

The young worker only made the remark about how lucky Beth had been not to have had to work yet in her life, but otherwise, a social security card was issued without question.

Beth appeared next at the tag agency. Nelson had been waiting for her and went to the counter to wait on her himself. His man who gave the driving test was there on Mondays. She passed with flying colors, of course, and also aced the written test.

After all, it was the same state, so she already knew the rules, the point system, and all that. So, the photo for the license had Beth with short, darkish-brown hair and glasses. She did not smile in the photo, so no one could recognize that, the smile that had always come so readily and beautifully to her.

But not right now.

Uncle Nelson handled the whole procedure himself, as he did sometimes with customers, so it was not an obvious thing.

It was just a routine issue.

There was no resemblance to Misee Sue Stone, and that was the idea.

When Beth returned to the car where Gail and Barbara were waiting, they couldn't contain their excitement.

A special lunch was in order.

Beth looked out the car window on the way to the restaurant, which Barbara and Gail were discussing and deciding on.

She couldn't believe her luck. Or, did more than luck come into play with this? She didn't know. Only briefly, did a shadow of sorrow cross her face.

Misee Sue Stone was definitely no more.

Chapter 19

K ia?"

"Yes, Grandma?" Kia answered. She saw who it was on her caller ID.

"Want to help me with a mission, just between you, me, and the fence post?"

Grandma always used that expression when she wanted something to remain between the two of them. There had been many occasions for that—an illegal ice cream cone before a meal, but Kia always managed to eat the full meal, anyway, so her mom never suspected anything. And there were other occasions on which Grandma spoiled them.

If the parents knew or suspected, they never said anything to either of them. Grandma had done these types of things all their lives. This was bound to be something good!

Besides, in the last two weeks since Misee Sue had

been gone, Kia and Grandma were closer than ever. They both had always believed Misee Sue had told the truth about catching that ball.

Although it had come to light through Latimer Jones that Misee Sue *had* told the truth, they didn't say anything to anyone, except themselves, that they had always believed her.

"We're not saying a word about this to anyone, but how would you like to help me cut down that stupid Wilson bush?"

"Are you serious? You bet," Kia replied. "I would like nothing better than to see that dam—sorry, darn—thing come down. And I'm not the only one. How are we going to do this? What's your plan?"

Kia was excited. She knew her grandma would have a great idea. This would partially vindicate Misee Sue, though it would not bring her back.

Misee Sue had been gone for two weeks and two days now, but no one but Kia knew about the two days. And she wasn't going to say a word.

"Your dad has a hand saw, doesn't he, out in the garage? I thought I saw one once, that one about three feet long, but for one person to use?"

"Yeah, I know the one you mean," Kia replied.

"Okay," Grandma continued, "can you, at some point, take that outside and hide it next to the house, maybe on the solid side of the garage? There are no windows there. Does your dad go on that side of the house very often?"

"I can't remember ever seeing him there. The lawn guys do the lawn. They trim all the bushes between us and the side fence. I can put the saw between the bushes and the garage on that side. Well, depending on when you want to cut down that bush. The lawn guys come in two days, again. It's their regular time."

"That's a good deal, because I'd like you to sneak out of the house tonight, around midnight, when you know everyone is asleep, get the saw, walk to my house to meet me, and we'll take the shortcut to the back of the center field. We'll have to go through Latimer's yard beside the barn, but his dog died last week, so we shouldn't have to worry about anything there. I'll have a saw, also. I just want that thing cut down."

As her grandma talked, Kia grew more excited by the minute. She was certainly up for this. "No one will be home for a while right now," she said. "I'll go out there right now and hide the saw. I'll see you at midnight."

"Good deal, sweetheart. See you then."

Kia knew she wouldn't sleep. This would be a great adventure. Never again would a catch, or miss, as the case may be, by the center fielder, go unseen.

It was about time.

Chapter 20

The trip to center field went as planned—silent and swift. Kia lived farther away than her grandma, but she walked quicker, and she knew exactly, to the minute, how long it took to walk to her grandma's house. She let herself in the back door exactly at midnight.

"Let's go," Grandma said.

When they got to the field, they sawed at the branches. Then they heard a loud whisper that nearly scared them to death, as Grandma described it afterward.

They rose up.

"Susan Horner and Kia Stone, what are you two up to?"

They immediately thought they were in trouble, for sure.

It was Latimer.

"Well…huh…we're caught, I guess, aren't we?" Susan asked.

"It's okay, look what I brought to the party," Latimer said. He held up a good-sized hand saw, but he could handle it by himself. There was a full moon, so Susan and Kia saw it plainly.

"But you're going about it the wrong way," Latimer began. "Here's a better plan…"

He had them go to either side of the bush and then hold on to the larger inner branches to steady the whole thing.

He would saw off the main trunk and then place it alongside the stump that was left. Hopefully, there was enough foliage all around to keep the sawed-off bush upright, giving it the appearance of still being there, hale and hearty. That was one thing about this darn bush through the years, it had simply grown and grown, never getting a disease or dying off.

Of course, this growth was helped in the dry seasons by the Better Garden and Lawn Society of the town. Several ladies had made it their duty through the years to keep it watered, even to the extent of carrying the water to it in buckets. This happened the year Latimer did not have a hose that went from his outside pump to the field. Otherwise, they used his back well. Latimer had been on the town's water supply for years, but also had a well to water the livestock that the farm had originally produced.

The well sported a hand pump, and years later, an electric pump to the faucet. This way, there was no water charge to keep the bush healthy.

"Good thing this isn't a holly bush," Susan murmured under her breath, but the other two heard her.

The branches were scratchy enough, but the two ladies held on tight.

When the deed was done, Latimer motioned for the ladies to come back to the barn. They made sure nothing was left behind, no evidence. He led them through the back door, the same door he had stepped out of just in time to see Misee Sue make her miraculous catch. Once inside, he turned on the light. There were no outside windows in this inner room, so they had no fear of being seen.

"So, here's my idea," he began. "We never, and I mean *never*, say a word about this to anyone, ever. Not for the rest of our lives. This is Wednesday. Next Wednesday the Better Yard and Garden Society meets at the bush for their annual homage to the bush, plus Joe is coming to trim it."

Joe was Joe Brown of Joe's Yard & Tree Trimming Service. Most of the locals used him for trimming their trees and shrubs.

"As you know," Latimer continued, "I'm a member, keeping up my mom's yard and garden that she was so proud of for so many years of her life, plus the fact that she was president of that silly group for more years than I can remember."

The two ladies nodded. Everyone knew that and didn't think it was strange at all for a man to be a member of the garden club. In fact, there was one more man who was a member.

"Since I'm the treasurer, I'll join the ladies at the bush. There shouldn't be any activity in the ball field in the next week. Most people are taking vacations. If someone notices the leaves are dying, I'll notice it, also, and then walk around it, inspecting it. Even if no one else notices the leaves, I'll bring it up as a question, like, 'Doesn't this bush look a little dry? Are the leaves dying?' The ladies won't think a thing about it. As I inspect it, I'll notice the trunk has been sawed totally off and sitting beside the stump. I'll be appropriately surprised and outraged, of course. Then I'll suggest that Joe take the stump out, roots and all, fill the hole, and then tamp it down and make the whole thing level. Another plan I'll suggest is that the club put a plague on a stand just inside the main entrance to the stadium with a rope around and all, with complete history of Henry Wilson giving his generous donation of land for the ball park, setting up a trust to maintain it for many years, and all that. This will all be a spur-of-the-moment idea, of course. Now, you both know that Cynthia will probably protest at first, say they'll have to think about it but probably come back a week later, making it all her plan and taking credit for the idea."

Again, they nodded.

They knew Cynthia Smithe—who always corrected people who said her name, making sure they knew the last name was pronounced "Smithe," with a long "i" instead of the usual "Smith." That was just too common for her. The old timers, of course, remembered a time when the name *was* the usual "Smith." Most townspeople just shook their heads at her.

Behind her back, of course.

"Latimer, what a great plan!" Susan exclaimed. "I didn't know you had it in you to think of something like that."

She laughed as Kia smiled.

"And I wouldn't have thought you had it in you, or Kia, to sneak around at midnight and cut down that bush. Anyway, I've been thinking about cutting down that tree myself, and then when I saw you two sneaking past the house with saws, I guessed immediately what you were up to. It took about two seconds for me to decide to join you. I know we did it in honor of Misee Sue. At least we had to make sure no other catch can be contested. Everyone should be able to see the center field very well.

Susan looked at her granddaughter. "We won't ever say a word about this, will we, Kia?"

Kia drew her fingers across her lips like a zipper.

And they didn't.

The plaque, on a stand, went up at the main entrance to the stadium, engraved with a picture of the bush and a history of Mr. Henry Wilson and his importance to the town. It was placed where all coming into the stadium, after paying their admission fee, could stop, admire it, and read about it, if they chose.

All the ladies of the Better Yard and Garden Society agreed later that it was much better than the small plaque by the bush and better, even, than just having that bush there all by itself.

Chapter 21

That Saturday, after Joe had done his work on Thursday of smoothing the ground where the bush had been, six teenaged boys showed up at the far edge of the field by the stands.

They were talking and laughing as they came on the field.

All of a sudden, one of them stopped, causing the one behind him to run into him.

"What's your problem, man?" the one behind asked.

"Look!" Kaden said, pointing.

They all looked in the direction Kaden pointed. It took all of them a few seconds to comprehend what they were *not* seeing.

"It's gone!" Steven exclaimed. "The Wilson Bush is gone! I can't believe it."

They all jogged out to center field. They stood looking at the hard-packed, flat area where the bush had been.

One of the boys spied Latimer, who was working on his lathe at the back of his barn. He was sharpening the saw he had used to cut down the bush.

"Mr. Jones," Steven called. The boys waved. They started jogging toward him.

Latimer looked up. He waved. He casually placed the saw, flat, at the back of the lathe and put a rag over it. He walked to another workbench and had his hand on top of a large vise connected to the end of the bench by the time the boys arrived.

Kaden pointed in the direction of the center field. "Mr. Jones, have you seen that?"

"Yep, that's something, isn't it?" Latimer responded.

"Did you see who did it? Who cut down the bush? We haven't heard anything about it," one of the boys asked.

"The ladies of the Garden Society met at the bush last week. One of them saw it had been cut off at the stump. They called Joe to come dig out the roots and fill in the hole."

He told the truth. That was what happened.

"Wow! I bet those old ladies were furious. Mom says nothing was more important to them than that dumb bush. Did you see who did it?"

The question was asked again.

"This old barn of mine is directly in front of my

house and the ball field. I have to come out here to see anything."

In their excitement, they didn't notice that Mr. Jones never answered the question. They seemed satisfied that he couldn't see from his house.

"I think it's great, especially now. 'Course, it's too late for Misee Sue, but it's sure great now. Hey, I'm going to call some of the other teams, let them know it's gone. They'll be as happy as we are, I bet. Let's go throw some balls around," one of the boys said.

They looked at Mr. Jones, who had casually moved so the view was totally opposite the lathe. Their attention would focus on the other workbench, if at all.

"See you, sir," several said, as they turned away.

"Enjoy, fellas," Latimer called back.

He went into his barn by the back door and closed it. He didn't want them to look back this way and see him sharpening a saw. That saw would be there when he wanted it.

⌘

From then on, through the years, whenever the subject of The Bush came up, anywhere, Latimer, Susan, and Kia just listened. They never made a comment unless someone asked a question directly of them, maybe what they thought of it.

They answered with "That was really something, wasn't it?" or something to that effect.

They never lied about it. They weren't liars about anything.

They just never told the whole truth about it.

Chapter 22

Beth went out early each morning to ride horses with Brian. By the end of the week, one particular horse, named Star, decided Beth belonged to her. She came when she saw Beth, while the others did not.

Brian asked her if she wanted to ride Star every time she came, and they agreed that she could do that.

Brian laughed. "She thinks you belong to her, so we might as well go with it."

Beth and Brian became the best of friends during that first week. They both felt they had known each other from the first time they met, but this riding and talking, sharing their lives, and laughing together sealed a lasting friendship.

Every day after riding each morning, Beth went back

to Gail's house to shower, change and visit several shops that had more than one employer/owner.

They let her fill out applications as they talked with her, learned a little—as much as she wanted them to learn—of her background, and the fact that she planned to stay in this small town.

It was so unusual that a girl her age wanted to stay, they were amazed. They would certainly keep her in mind when they needed an employee.

She didn't get discouraged, not with Brian encouraging her each morning. She had enough money to carry her for quite a while. But she didn't want Gail and Barbara to think she planned to live with them forever. They all had discussed that, and it was understood, but there was no great rush for her to move out, either. She had the room and private bath that had belonged to Barbara's grandmother, who had passed on, so there was plenty of room.

She was sitting on the back patio late Friday afternoon, where her new life had all started it seemed, when she received a call from Brian.

He was excited. He was at the library. He had just found out from Miss Betty, the librarian, that her only employee, her assistant, had suddenly given notice, that this afternoon, right now, was her last day. There had been no former, proper notice.

Miss Betty was beside herself. She had forgotten that Beth had been in on Tuesday, but Brian did not forget.

He had really kept his ears open for any chance of a job for Beth.

"Miss Betty says, can you come in right now and talk to her, with me here?" he asked.

Beth's feet, which had been up on the table in front of her, had already hit the floor. "Of course, I'll be right there."

"Good deal. We'll be here."

She called Gail, to tell her what was happening, and that she might be late picking her up. Gail didn't mind. She could grab a coffee at the Starbucks across the street from her office. She was just happy for Beth. The library seemed ideal for her.

Gail worked over in the county seat at a law firm. Beth had been driving her to work each morning, doing what she needed to do during the day, and then picking Gail up after work.

Beth took a few seconds to change to slacks. She knew shorts were not appropriate for a job interview.

To her surprise, Miss Betty hired her on the spot. She even asked Beth to come back the next morning to read to the children, and Beth agreed to.

When all the paperwork was settled, Miss Betty had one more question.

"I know you're staying with Barbara and the family, but would you be interested in having your own place? Just an apartment, mostly furnished? Not only did this whole situation leave me without a helper, or so I thought—" She smiled at Beth. "—but it also has left a friend of mine—you know Clarissa Adams, don't you, Brian?"

Brian nodded. He just saw where Miss Betty was going with this.

"Well," Miss Betty continued, "Janice also rented her apartment. I bet everything is already cleaned out of there. I bet Clarissa is in shock right now. She always depended on the extra income from that garage apartment to help her get by. As far as I know, her only other income is the amount she gets from Robert's social security check each month. And that's not a lot, I don't suppose. Shall I call her?"

Beth agreed, of course. A small garage apartment sounded just fine to her. She pictured a large, efficiency-type room, on top of a garage, with stairs going up the side of the garage, which would give her some good exercise. She was young, and it was just her. Anything would do.

Miss Betty hung up the phone. "Clarissa says, can you come right over? I was right; Janice was already packed and ready to go when she told Clarissa she was leaving. Clarissa says she hasn't even had a chance to see what shape Janice left the apartment in, but you are welcome to come and look at it. I know she would rent it to you if you want it. Clarissa also said she watched Janice get into a sporty-looking car with a not-so-young man she didn't know."

She looked at Brian first, then at Beth.

This is where the gossip in a small town comes into play, Beth thought. *Miss Betty is hoping we will know who the man is and tell her.*

Beth didn't know, though, being so new in town. They both looked at Brian.

"I have no idea," he said. "I haven't been in town so much this time of year. The baling and everything."

Miss Betty nodded. She understood, but she had hoped he knew who it was. It would be good gossip for the next week or so. Janice was born there, one of their own, but she had always been restless, wanting to be out of this small town, wanting to live in the big city where she could simply "do" more.

It seems she found her opportunity. All three agreed they hoped the best for her. Sometimes these situations did not work out, and the young lady came home, a little worse for wear, but wiser in the ways of the world. Her small town looked better at that point.

Beth knew Brian well enough, in this short week, to know that he would not have told Miss Betty anything, even if he had known something about Janice's situation. He just wasn't like that.

With the simple directions—"Go two blocks that way, turn left, and it's the last house on the right, on the corner. You can't miss it. It has large peony bushes around it"—to guide her, Beth walked the three blocks from the library to Miss Clarissa's house quite easily.

She approached from what was the back of the main house. There was a driveway off this street, leading to a single-car detached garage which opened toward the side. The part where the car parked was only half the structure. The other half had an outside walk-in door and had been originally built as an apartment as part of the whole structure. A cute little porch had been built to protect the front door. A window above the garage part indicated a room there.

Beth walked around to the front of the house, which faced another street. Since Miss Clarissa was expecting her, she was sitting on the swing on her front porch. "What a mess this is, isn't it?" she began. "But if you need an apartment, this is going to work out best for everyone. You can certainly walk to the library from here, even in bad weather. Betty said you did not have a car of your own yet, that you've been living with Barbara. Come on in. We can get to the apartment better by going through the house."

No formal introduction was made. Beth had noticed in this small town that everyone seemed to be on a first-name, familiar basis from the beginning of a relationship. Also, every woman beyond a certain age was "Miss So-and-So."

She would become Miss Beth to the children.

The apartment was a surprise. The main floor was an open area consisting of a nice-sized living space/eat-in kitchen combination with a back door. There was also a door leading to the garage part, so a person could enter the apartment in bad weather without getting wet or whatever. Under the stairs, there was a full-sized bathroom, with a full shower, no bathtub. Miss Clarissa said no one took baths anymore, anyway, and showers saved water.

They went up the stairs, which were built on the garage side of the living room, flush with the wall. On the left was the "master," as Miss Clarissa called it. It was a large bedroom with a private bath. Across the hall was another bedroom over the garage. This was the window she had seen from the street.

The master had a full bed, night stand, dresser, and chest of drawers, a matching set. The second bedroom was empty. Miss Clarissa said she had never had the need to furnish it. Mainly single ladies had lived there. She said the living room had a regular-sized sleeper sofa, anyway, which guests could sleep on, use the downstairs bath.

Everything was furnished, including linens. The kitchen was equipped with a four-place setting of everything needed to eat a meal, plus pots and pans to cook with. There were potholders, dishcloths, and dish towels.

"If something you need is not here, until you start getting paid and can buy whatever you want, then just let me know. I have extra of everything in the house, have had since the children were here. I've never had the heart to throw away all those memories. But, the linens and things are still good and clean, you wouldn't have to worry about that."

"This is all I need and more," Beth answered, "I just hope I can afford it. How much is it per month?"

She knew she had plenty for whatever security deposit was asked, but she wanted to be able to pay the rent out of her regular salary at the library, which was only a couple of dollars per hour above minimum wage. She certainly had taken the job when it was offered to her, though. She had seen this week that jobs came at a premium in this town.

"How about two hundred fifty dollars a month? Is that too much?"

Beth couldn't believe her ears. Only $250 a month?

"You would pay your own utilities, of course, but there is no deposit on that. They're in my name but under this address. When the bill comes in, I'll just bring it to you, and you can pay it. There's a landline, of course. Same setup for payment. But if you want cable TV, Wi-Fi, you'll have to be on your own for that. The apartment is cable ready, though, so you just have to get service in your name. Oh, and there's a two hundred fifty-dollar security deposit. And, no loud music or parties, young men staying over or anything like that. I don't go for that sort of thing. Can you live with that?"

Beth certainly could live with that. She'd had enough of sneaking to parties and facing her parents' wrath to last her lifetime. "Don't worry. There'll be nothing like that.

I'll take it, of course," Beth said. "It's perfect for me, and, as you said, it's so close to the library. I don't have the five hundred dollars on me right now, how about tomorrow?"

"Done and done," Miss Clarissa said. "I'll be home all day. I'll give you the key as soon as you 'show me the money.'"

Miss Clarissa laughed at the reference to the movie.

They set a time for Beth to be there tomorrow.

She walked back to the library on "Cloud 9." She really couldn't believe her luck. Finding a job and an apartment all in the same afternoon. The gods were certainly smiling down at her. This was certainly the place, the town, she was meant to live in.

Who could ask for anything more?

∾∾

After several months, Miss Clarissa asked Beth if she would like to come over that evening to watch her favorite TV show with her. A new season was starting.

Beth agreed, and they had a good evening together.

By the next week, Miss Clarissa asked if Beth would like to come to dinner before the show started, and then they could watch together.

Beth agreed.

This was Thursday, an evening when the library closed early. This became a weekly routine for Miss

Clarissa and Beth. They became good friends, not just landlady and tenant. It didn't matter that Miss Clarissa was old enough, and then some, to be Beth's mother. Their friendship had no age limits.

After the show, they would sit on the front porch and wave and speak to various people as they walked their dogs for the evening. Miss Clarissa introduced Beth to many of the townspeople that way, who then came into the library at various times during the week to chat a few minutes more.

Beth settled in quite nicely in Evansville. No one seemed to mind her age, or ask questions. They just accepted her for who she was. Her smile seemed to light up the room or brighten their day.

And why shouldn't she settle in nicely? This town was only a little bigger than her hometown, and she had always been satisfied there. She had never wanted to go to the big city to make more money or be famous, or anything else.

Her heart was in this town now.

Chapter 23

Beth had been at the library for several months. It was the end of the summer, with only one more week before school started. That meant there would be just one more Children's Reading Time on Wednesday at the library.

Miss Betty had given Beth free rein to choose what books she wanted to read. These came as a result of Beth going through every child's book in the library on her free time, but she wanted to know what was there.

She found several books she could read to a child, which were real classics. They were hidden in the midst of other books.

One morning, she had put a display of the books in one of the library windows with an outside view. The display was quite attractive and eye-catching. Now, she was cleaning the window and sill on the outside.

She looked up when she sensed two people had stopped behind her. She turned around.

"Well, good morning, Billy, how are you this morning? And this is…"

"Hi, Miss Beth, and this is my mom, Sharon."

"I'm so glad to meet you, Sharon, Billy's mom. He is such a joy to have in story time."

"Thanks, Miss Beth," Billy replied.

"He likes you so much and looks forward to the story time every week. I think most of us mothers are glad you came to the library," Sharon responded.

"Miss Beth?" Billy asked. He had been looking in the window. "I've never seen that book before. May I check it out when it comes out of the window?"

"You may check it out anytime you like," Beth replied.

"Really? Right now?" Billy asked, eagerly.

"Of course, just go in and see Miss Betty. She'll get it for you."

"Wow!" Billy replied.

As he went in, Sharon and Beth chatted. In a few seconds, an arm appeared and took the book away, along with a small face right beside it. Miss Betty and Billy waved to them through the window.

In a few minutes, Billy was out with the book.

"Gee, thanks, Miss Beth," he said.

"Anytime, Billy. You can check out any book in the library, anytime. Never be afraid to ask for it, either from Miss Betty or me."

"See you," they both said, as they turned to walk away. Beth went back to washing the window.

She became a much-beloved librarian through the years and a true favorite of the children. She saw by the books available that the library could use more children's resources, so she bought two books or items a month as long as she worked there. Miss Betty said she didn't have to—the library had a budget for that. But, after seeing the amount available, Beth was glad to do it. This way, the children always had something new each month for story time and to check out.

Chapter 24

Clayton arrived on the university campus early on the first day of matriculation. The campus police had agreed to look for Misee Sue. Carrying an enlarged photo of her senior picture, they were all out in force all over the campus. Clayton stationed himself just inside the main entrance to the gym, where they both would have enrolled. Computers were set up for the students on tables. They would enroll online at this time.

He missed signing up for a class he wanted in particular, because the professor had been recommended. Later in the day, when he realized Misee Sue was not going to be there, he left his post to enroll. He was able to get the same class, just a different professor, but, as it turned out, it was for the best. The former was asked to leave in disgrace, during that first semester, and the latter became a good, lifelong friend. Clayton only realized that years later, of course.

The campus police kept up a vigil for the next two weeks, but when the last day to enroll for the semester ended, they said they would have to call it quits.

Misee Sue had given up her opportunity to go to university, at least this semester. Every semester from then on, Clayton watched for her, but to no avail.

They all hated to admit it, but the chief of police might have been right in the first place. Since the car had never turned up anywhere, and of course the license ran out that next year and was never renewed, they agreed there must have been foul play involved.

They would probably never see Misee Sue again. Misee Sue would never know it, but her mom silently grieved from that point on for what she had done to her beautiful, intelligent daughter, her first-born.

Her mom would die of a broken heart.

Chapter 25

From the first time Beth read for the children during Children's Time at the library, the very next day she was hired, she loved it, and they all seemed to love her. The parents were very supportive. Miss Betty had already made plans for that Saturday, so Beth was thrust into the reading at last minute. But it worked out.

The schedule became that Miss Betty worked one Saturday and Beth the next. That way, they each had two weekends off a month for personal time. The relationship between the two of them became one of best friends as well as coworkers.

Fortunately, the trust that provided the salary for an extra person continued through the years.

One thing Beth wanted to work on was the fact that this small library still used an old wooden card catalog system. The Dewey Decimal System would never change, of course, but the little cards had given way to computers in most libraries. The Online Public Access Catalog was the modern system. This small town and library had not been able to afford a computerized patron system for checking in and out books, or looking up access for many things. The library was part of the state system for ebooks, and several great online databases, but just did not have all the state-of-the art equipment it needed. Miss Betty had presented several items to the town council for its consideration, with the understanding that if the town ever had any extra funds, there was a need for this.

The school had a grant providing for Google Chrome tablets for each grade. The grants writer volunteered to write and send grants, both to the federal government and to private organizations. The town wasn't as sleepy as Beth feared. There were many progressive programs here.

Beth approached Miss Betty one day with the idea that she, Beth, would like to buy and donate a new system to the library. She had just enough extra funds for one, and, for right now, that would be enough for the town. The townspeople were extremely grateful. Beth scheduled sessions to train adults and children alike how to access everything.

They settled on the Atriuum Information Library System. It would be browser-based, giving patrons instant access to all resource material at the library from any internet connected computer mobile device. A good system would provide the Atriuum on the Goapplication for several smart phones.

Not only Miss Betty and Beth, but also all patrons could use the app to access the library catalog and search or items by ISBN or barcode. She would have a good time putting the correct barcode on the 8,000-plus books that didn't have them. Once connected, they could reserve or renew books, read reviews, use trending items, and more.

It would take a while, but she wasn't going anywhere, anyway.

When they found out the cost of the new system, and asked the town council to help Beth with the cost, one man stepped up to donate the whole amount. His children had grown up using this library and were now in great positions in their chosen fields. He knew this little library had a lot to do with their education. He could afford it, also.

Beth was secretly grateful. She had the money, yes, but now she could use it longer for things she needed.

Time passed quickly.

Beth became a town favorite in the next three years she lived here. The library position was fine with her as was her not-so-small garage apartment. She had been able to purchase a good, used car from a young man who worked at Dale's Auto Body. He did excellent body work. The car had been totally refurbished by Dale himself, so it worked out for both of them.

She had never needed to go farther than the next town over, which was the county seat. What clothes and shoes she needed more than she had moved there with, she ordered online and never had to return anything. She guessed she was just a common size!

Gail was still a best friend, as Brian had become. There were other friends, and she was glad to have a group to do things with, but these three became their own best friends. At first, some asked the usual questions of why she had moved there, but seemed satisfied when she said she needed to move away from her home and start a new life. Most pictured physical or mental abuse, so they didn't question further. They simply accepted her and her winning ways.

If there were some who thought it was odd that she and Brian had lunch and dinner together occasionally, nothing was said, except one time, when an older woman asked if they were "serious." With a straight face, Brian assured her they were just the best of friends. She accepted that and moved on.

Then they looked at each other and smiled.

He laughed. "I guess we will always seriously be friends, or serious friends, or friends that are serious—whatever."

"Of course, but may we laugh and have fun on occasion?" Beth asked.

"Sure, in fact, why don't we plan a weekend getaway somewhere? Just a little road trip?"

Beth looked seriously at Brian. "We both know that, even if we get a room with double beds, that would be okay, right?"

"I knew you knew," Brian returned. He smiled at his friend.

"I've known since that day you hid the car for me. I also knew we would be best friends. And, aren't we?"

"Oh, most definitely," Brian assured her. "I don't think most people in town suspect anything, though, do you?"

"No, I don't, and is there a reason you don't want them to know?"

He just shrugged. "My parents both knew, so I guess that was good enough for me. I respected the fact that they had many friends in town that didn't agree with me, so I've kept quiet. I think it's just always been like the old military, a 'don't ask, don't tell' policy on my part. It's no one's business."

"I agree, but don't you get lonely living by yourself out on that farm? You've been the best man for two weddings since I've lived here. Doesn't that make you want more…companionship, let's say?" Beth asked.

Brian shrugged again. "So far, I've kept busy enough on the farm not to worry too much about it. Since I expanded, though, and hired the two guys I have, I do have more leisure time. That's why I suggested this road trip for us. I think we'd both enjoy it."

Gail had gone on to the university of her choice, so she was not around as much as she used to be. She was a junior at this point, her program proceeding as scheduled.

"Oh, for sure," Beth agreed.

They made plans. To the big city they would go!

It was the end of Beth's third year in Evansville.

Chapter 26

Kia had settled in the dorm for her first year at university. This was her third week there. She had been "rushed" during Greek Week, but on second thought, she decided to go into the dorm. The Greek life just didn't seem right for her.

There was a frat party tonight that she had been invited to, but she chose to reread a paper that she had written that was due on Monday. She wanted to make sure it said exactly what she wanted it to say.

When her phone rang, she answered it with her left hand. It was her habit to *not* answer and refuse the call if she didn't recognize the number. She would not have recognized this number, but she was concentrating so hard on her paper, she answered automatically.

"Hello?"

"Well, I hope you're in your dorm room, studying away, and *not* at a kegger."

At the first word, Kia's eyes flew open. By the third word, her right hand was at her heart. "Misee Sue? Oh, Misee Sue, is that really you? Really? I can't believe it!"

"It's me, Kia, darling. I waited until I knew you were at university before I contacted you. That way it was safe. No one else needs to know. I'm just glad you have the same phone number."

"Misee Sue, where are you? Can I see you? When? Where?" Kia was so excited, she wanted to ask everything at once.

"What are you doing tomorrow?" Beth asked. "Are you willing to drive a couple of hours?"

Beth was counting on the fact that the parents had probably given Kia a new car for her high school graduation, just as they had her.

"Yes, of course, to see you, I'll come anywhere. Where?"

Beth named a town that she knew was about two hours from the university, though a little farther for her. They agreed on a time and place.

Beth impressed on Kia the need to keep the trip secret, and Kia agreed not to say a word to anyone.

Beth drove to the town the night before and stayed at the Hampton Inn overnight. She also rented a car, so her own would not be seen here, for any reason, by any one.

She knew the walls had ears, and the night a thousand eyes! In this case, the day!

She trusted Kia but wasn't ready yet to tell her everything about the last three years. Maybe she would someday, but not just now.

As she put a few items on a plate at the breakfast buffet the inn provided, she felt happy at the thought of seeing Kia. Only Kia, she realized. She wasn't worried about anyone else. She had no feelings toward them. She didn't judge herself or wonder whether having no feelings was right or wrong.

That's just the way it was.

Even with a rental car, Beth parked a couple of blocks from the fast-food restaurant where they were to meet. As she walked around the building, Kia saw her out the window and met her at the door, jumping up and down.

It took Beth several minutes to calm down Kia. She didn't want to draw attention to them. You never knew when someone would remember something. They ordered something so they could sit there as long as they wanted to.

"You look so wonderful, Misee Sue, except for the glasses and hair, of course, but I would know you anywhere. But why did you cut your hair? Oh, of course, you don't want to be recognized, do you? We never thought about dark hair and glasses, although we thought perhaps you might cut your hair. But glasses! You look nothing like your poster…that reminds me, you need to know…"

"No!" Beth said adamantly. She held up her hand, palm toward Kia, at the same time. "Stop!"

Kia looked puzzled. "Don't you want to know about the last three years?"

"No, I really don't. I don't want to hear anything about our hometown, or anyone in it, and I mean *any-one*!"

Beth said it so emphatically, Kia was speechless. But she saw in Misee Sue's eyes a hardness, a look of steel that told Kia the hurt and humiliation of the whole situation and treatment Misee Sue had received from everyone was still there and that Misee Sue would never relive it, not in thought or memories. Kia hoped that all those memories were there, just that Misee Sue had tucked them so far away they wouldn't surface again for a while. Maybe someday they could talk about everything.

The talk would not occur until their old age, Kia just didn't know it at this time.

Beth was looking at Kia without blinking, stone-faced. This hardness in her eyes, this face, was entirely new to Kia. She never saw this in her gentle, kind-hearted older sister before.

Kia's heart jumped. Where was her Misee Sue?

Then suddenly, it seemed like the old Misee Sue was back.

She gave Kia a gentle smile and continued in a soft

voice. "Let's go from here, Kia, darling, okay? Let's make our own memories from this day on."

Kia relaxed. The sparkle was back in Misee Sue's eyes and the kind, gentle voice she remembered and knew so well had returned.

"Now," Beth began, "tell me about your high school days. You are so beautiful now, so mature. You were pretty, of course, in the ninth grade, with so much potential, and look at you now. You've certainly grown up!"

Kia laughed. She wasn't ready to describe to Misee Sue how she found Misee Sue, not that look she had seen a minute ago in those eyes. Misee Sue was definitely changed, that was for sure, but Kia knew that was not all bad.

They only had time during that first meeting to relive Kia's tenth grade, but it had been a happy time for Kia.

"Except for your not being there, of course," Kia was quick to say. She didn't want Misee Sue to think she had forgotten her, not even for a second, during that time or any time after that.

"I'm here now," Beth replied. She made no apologies for not being there overall, but did tell Kia she hated to miss out on her high school years and graduation. "But chances are, being in college, I would not have had much time with you, anyway, so cheer up!"

"Oh, so you did go to college somewhere. Clayton and everyone looked for you that first day—"

Again, the hand up to stop Kia. "I told you not to talk

about anything from that time or ever, and I meant it, Kia. If you're going to try to tell me something every time we see each other, then we just won't see each other. That's the way it has to be." Again, that voice and those eyes of steel.

"I'm sorry, I forgot," Kia apologized. "Of course, I want to see you forever now! I'll remember."

Again, the return of the old Misee Sue smile.

They agreed to meet here, in this town, every other Saturday. This worked out well with Beth's schedule at the library.

This became their routine. After three months, when Beth knew she could trust Kia to keep her word, she asked Kia to bring their grandmother.

Susan couldn't stop crying when she saw Misee Sue. She talked so fast, she got it in that they all thought for sure Misee Sue had met a horrible death at the hands of a kidnapper or rapist.

Kia and Grandma swore silence. Seeing Misee Sue would be their secret. They would respect her wishes.

Chapter 27

For the next year during Kia's freshman year, which was Clayton's senior year, whenever they happened to meet each other on campus, they stopped and chatted for a moment or two. They had different majors, so were not in the same buildings on campus, one usually on one end, and the other on the other end, but occasionally they crossed paths. Neither one brought up the subject of Misee Sue, just general topics, maybe something one or the other had heard from their hometown.

Clayton always had the feeling that Kia blamed him, at least partially, maybe the majority, for Misee Sue leaving home.

He was not wrong. Kia *did* blame him. He had loved Misee Sue, she was sure of that. Even in her fifteen-year-old way at the time, she had seen the love. But how could a person say they love you and turn your back on you like that? So, yes, she blamed Clayton in lots of ways.

Kia, on her part, always had the urge to tell him about Misee Sue, how they met every other week and that Misee Sue looked so good and was doing well. She wanted to tell him everything. But she never did, of course. A promise was a promise.

In the middle of his sophomore year, he had finally told Marie just how he felt about her. Since Marie's words had been the main reason no one had believed Misee Sue about catching the ball, Clayton had never forgiven her.

She, on the other hand, had hoped to replace Misee Sue in Clayton's heart. The first year, during the summer at home, and now, for the first semester of this year, she had called him, followed him around, and even made sure she appeared in the same group of friends and places he was.

He had finally had enough. He turned to her and told her, in front of others, that if she didn't quit following him around, he would call the police and report her as a stalker. Several of his friends had noticed her following him, even watching his apartment window at night from across the street, so they told him they would be witnesses to him telling her to back off.

He told her she was not Misee Sue, would never be Misee Sue, and could never take the place of Misee Sue, so to forget it and leave him alone. It was not in his nature to be so mean to anyone, but she had never taken his subtle rejections seriously. He had to be more drastic.

She looked shocked but had no choice. This was a final humiliation in front of others. Since this was the end of the semester, she did not come back to the university in January. He heard from others that she had transferred to another college. He was just glad she did not do anything in retaliation. You know, the old "hell hath no jury like a woman scorned." He watched his back for a while.

Clayton graduated at the end of Kia's freshman year. Kia spent that first summer as a camp counselor, so she was gone more than she was home. She heard from her parents that he went back to their hometown to be the athlete coach and a teacher. Coach had retired suddenly at the end of the year. It was time.

Clayton returned to the small town, hoping deep in his heart to one day see Misee Sue, that she would come home.

How wrong he was.

Chapter 28

Tickets to a Broadway show were the highlight of Beth and Brian's visit to New York City. That would be tomorrow night.

Right now, they sat in a very crowded, Jewish deli in the heart of the city. They had been lucky to get a table for three against the wall. Beth had the famous Reuben and Brian the pastrami on rye. It was all they could do to eat it all, but they did. It was such a treat.

Beth was looking at Brian when his eyes went wide. She followed his glance. There was an attractive, light-brown-haired young lady looking at Brian. Then the young lady's attention went to the clerk behind the counter. She was about to receive her food. Beth looked back at Brian, who excused himself to go to the men's room. He quickly disappeared.

Beth did not mistake the look between the two. She knew what she saw.

The young lady started looking around the crowded room for a place to sit, but there were no spare tables.

Without thinking about it, Beth held up her hand as the woman glanced her way. Beth signaled her over. She weaved her way through the tables.

"This place is a real zoo," Beth began, "there's no way you're going to find a seat. Why don't you sit here with us? We have a third chair. You might as well sit before someone else claims it for their table."

She smiled, and the young lady smiled back. She sat down and started to unwrap her food.

"First of all, let's get something straight," Beth said to her.

She looked up, raising her eyebrows. She was surprised at such a statement from a stranger. "What's that?" she asked. She didn't know what to expect.

"If you break Brian's heart, I will find a way to hurt you, really bad. Brian is a best friend, and I won't have him hurt."

The woman was startled. She started to protest, to pretend not to know what Beth was talking about, but she had noted that Beth saw the look that passed between her and Brian. "I promise," she said. "I will never break his heart or hurt him for any reason."

She said it so seriously to Beth. Then she laughed.

Beth laughed also. "I mean it," she said.

"I know you do, and so do I," she agreed. "By the way, my name is Kelly."

"Pleased to meet you, Kelly, my name is Beth."

"I think I shall call you Beth, the Protector."

They laughed again.

By that time, Brian was coming toward the table. Beth, who was facing that way, saw him hesitate slightly when he saw Kelly at their table, but ever so slightly.

As Brian took his seat, Beth said, "Brian, this is Kelly. She was in danger of having to stand and try to eat her…Reuben, is it?" She leaned over and looked at Kelly's sandwich. "I felt I just had to rescue her from such a fate. These Reubens are works of art. You simply can't rush them or eat one standing up."

"I'm Kelly, " Kelly said to Brian. "I would shake your hand, but, as you can see, mine is full of this to-die-for Reuben—a work of art, as Beth says."

"That's fine," Brian said. "It is impossible to try to put down and even more so to try to pick up again. I just see where I stand, that's all!"

Brian and Kelly smiled at each other.

Beth knew it was going to be perfect. "We're not from here, just your usual tourists. We heard about this place, but had no idea it would be this crowded."

"Yeah, it's enjoyed by tourists and locals alike. Where are you from and how long are you staying?" Kelly asked, between bites.

"Just for the next three days, I'm afraid. We have tickets to Broadway for tomorrow night, but, otherwise, we're just enjoying looking at everything. And, enjoying the wonderful food, of course. Do you live here?" Beth asked.

"No, I'm just here for a few days, also, but go back the day after tomorrow. I asked you first," she reminded them.

They gave the name of their small town in Kansas.

Kelly smiled. "It's a small world. I'm from Kansas, also." She said the name of her town, one only slightly bigger than theirs. "But I work in Lawrence, which is as big as I want to live in," she concluded.

"I know what you mean," Brian said. He had not said much, but Beth had noticed him stealing glances at Kelly Yes, they were very discreet, Beth just knew Brian so well that she could tell.

"And what do you do in Lawrence?" Beth asked.

They might as well all get to know each other. Why beat around the bush?

"I'm an attorney at one of the smaller law firms there, but we're growing. Our client base has reached the point that I came here to interview a couple of young attorneys who expressed interest in living in Lawrence. They both have family in that area, and they're looking to be near them. And you two? What do you do to afford a trip to the Big Apple?"

"I am a librarian, and Brian is a farmer," Beth answered.

Kelly looked from one to the other. She couldn't tell if Beth was really serious, or not.

"Really?" she asked. "I don't picture you as a librarian—" This she directed to Beth, and then she turned to Brian. "—or you as a farmer."

"All my life," Brian returned. "Well, I did go to university, but I majored in horticulture. I knew I would help my dad on the farm. I never wanted to do anything else. It's just that these days you have to be smart about it, understand the business and marketing ends of it, as well as just enjoy baling the hay."

"I would guess," Kelly said. "What do you produce on your farm? How big is it?" When Brian told her how big it was, and the extent of it, Kelly was wide-eyed. She laughed. "That's impressive, it really is, and here I immediately had a picture of a little farm with a few chickens and a milk cow by the barn."

Brian laughed, also. "I've never owned any chickens and never milked a cow. Mom had a Guernsey she liked to milk, but…" He couldn't finish his sentence at first but quickly recovered. "My parents were killed in a car accident six years ago, in the middle of my last semester at state. As I said, I knew I would take over the farm someday, but I thought it would be when Dad grew old and retired and just couldn't work it anymore. Little did I know it would be my responsibility at age twenty-seven. But here it is. And I wouldn't trade, or sell it, for anything else in the world."

As Brian talked about his parents, Kelly had reached out and put her hand over Brian's. Beth noticed that Brian did not pull his away but slowly turned it over so that they were holding hands. They each discreetly withdrew their hands when Brian finished.

"That wasn't fair, but I can tell you have handled it well—everything, I mean. I hope I see this farm someday."

"Of course," Brian said. He seemed surprised that it would be any other way.

They made plans to meet and see other places in the city together. Their hotels were not far from each other. Kelly would not be able to get a ticket to the play this late but would meet them afterward for a drink.

In the next two days, a love formed between Kelly and Brian. One was yet to admit it and would take a while, but one was sure. Beth was just as loved, she knew. This three-way friendship and love would last their lifetimes.

And this was only the end of Misee Sue's fourth year as Beth.

Chapter 29

Beth was sitting at her favorite place in the entire world. She definitely believed that. Comfortably ensconced on her favorite chair on Brian's back porch, she gazed at a beautiful sunset. She had a key to Brian's house, so she had gone to the kitchen and fixed herself a large glass of tea.

She did not know where Brian was, but that didn't matter. In the four years plus she had lived here and they had been friends, she came and went as she pleased at his farm. They were like brother and sister. She and Kelly had that same bond.

Although the back porch faced west, the sun was not on the porch at this time of day, thanks to a giant, majestic oak tree in the center of the yard, not far from the porch. It was so large and full, there was shade on this porch all day long. There were other trees, but this was, by far, the most magnificent one. Also, she had turned on the three ceiling fans on the porch when she arrived.

Presently, she saw Brian's pickup turn up the long drive off the highway. He pulled a cattle trailer behind it. He drove down to the barn, turned around and backed into a certain space before he got out.

"I see you've been to the sale barn again today," she said.

It was Wednesday. This part of the country always had cattle auctions at the sale barns on Wednesday. Beth had asked Brian if every sale barn had the cattle auction on the same day, how could you sell something in one place and buy something you wanted somewhere else on the same day? Brian had just laughed and said that's where friends came in. The cattle went into the pens at any given place that Monday or Tuesday and were cared for by the owners of the sale barn. If you saw something you wanted, you sent someone in your place, if you need-ed to be another place to sell your own stock. And there appeared to be different rates at different places. A few cents to a few dollars a pound here or there made a big difference when a five hundred, or whatever, pound cow was concerned.

"I guess you were selling today," she continued.

"Yeah," Brian answered. "Jake told me he is selling a few heifers next week, so I'll wait to buy then. At least, I hope to get the bid on them. They are prime stock, though, and just at breeding age. But you don't want to hear that. How about getting us some dinner while I shower and change? I could eat a horse." He laughed. "Or would that be a cow?"

She smiled as she went to the kitchen. There was a shower and extra clothes in Brian's mudroom. He would probably be changed by the time she put the food on a tray and took it to the porch. They had to enjoy this sunset. He still had Sam working for him, and she had learned to cook enough food for Beth, just in case she showed up to eat.

They were just into the salads when Brian spoke.

"I've invited Kelly to the farm for this coming weekend," he said. He said it casually, but Beth knew him well enough to know that he wanted her approval.

"It's about time," she answered with a smile.

Brian looked up, surprised. "What do you mean?"

"I meant just what I said. It's about time Kelly came here for a visit. You guys have been meeting somewhere else for the past year. It's time to come here and relax in your own space. Kelly will love it here. Does she ride?"

Beth took the announcement in stride, just as if it were a natural, normal occurrence.

"Yes, as a matter of a fact, she does, and thanks, I thought you might not approve. You know some in town would not—my dating a stranger, an outsider, and all."

"You know what I think about 'some' in town, although they will never know it, and you know you don't need my approval," Beth responded. "After all, two of us knew the minute we met that you and Kelly were meant to be together. It just took one of us longer to discover and admit it. Of course, for the past year or so, two out of three hasn't been bad, but it's time for the third person to be on board."

Brian's mouth was actually open. Then he grinned. "I know I knew immediately, also, but it had never happened to me before, and I'm twenty-seven years old, almost twenty-eight. I had to give it time and be completely certain about Kelly and what was happening between us."

"I know," Beth said, "and Kelly knew and gave you time and space. How does she feel about coming?"

"She's very excited, of course. I told her about the horses. She wanted to know if you could come and ride with us this Saturday morning."

"If it's early enough, of course, but it's my day to work. You know, Star is my horse, or I'm her person, whichever it is, but why don't we see if Leo accepts Kelly? Let's stand apart and see what happens."

Leo was the third horse, a large roan.

Saturday morning, Brian had the horses saddled, but they were out in the paddock, not at the fence.

When Star saw Beth, she started toward her, as did Homer to Brian. Leo held back, tossing his head. Kelly stood between the other two, with plenty of room for Leo to come to her. They pretended to ignore Leo.

It wasn't too many minutes, however, before Leo

came toward Kelly. He stopped a few feet from her and blew air through his nostrils. Kelly reached out her hand, let Leo take a few steps to touch her, and then she reached up and patted Leo's neck. A bond was formed, and that's what they had hoped for.

"Well, it looks like the three amigos are complete." Brian laughed. "I do miss Gail, however."

"Me, too," Beth echoed.

About six months previously, Gail had turned off the highway onto Brian's drive at faster-than-normal speed.

As usual, Beth and Brian were hanging out on the back porch.

"I wonder what her hurry is?" Beth had asked.

They soon found out. Gail was so excited. She had met what she claimed to be the best-looking man in the entire world. Beth and Brian had stolen a look at each other as Gail went into the kitchen to get some tea, still chatting about the man she met, only raising her voice so they still could hear her.

The two of them were sure it was the beginning of the end of their special friendship.

Or so they thought.

They were pleased when they met Matthew and loved him instantly. He was accepted into their circle without question. He felt the same way. They became the close friends he had never known growing up.

Gail and Matthew were to be married in a year. Matthew wanted time to establish his practice. Beth was to be the bridesmaid. Matthew asked Brian to be his best man. Why not? Gail and Brian had grown up together and were best friends.

Their engagement, of course, meant they saw less and less of Gail, although she still managed to come to ride every once in a while. Matthew wasn't comfortable with horses. When they were married, they were going to move to Wichita, where Matthew was one of four physicians in a budding family practice clinic.

Matthew was the one at the clinic that specialized in internal medicine. A practice in a town this size was not to be scoffed at. He could see three to four patients an hour, during the busy times, and that seemed to be every day, he said. Three of the four would probably be Medicare patients. After billing Medicare and maybe a supplement, one visit would be around $75. With four physicians in the practice, they could afford the four office personnel they had to pay. They had a young man who "did" the books, as he called it; one lady did their medical records, including coding; another billing, including Medicare; and the other two were out front, with patient access and scheduling.

A lab next door took care of their patients when blood tests were needed. All-in-all, Matthew was very happy to be there.

One main drawing feature, he said, was the fact that this area was determined by the Federal government to be demographically low income, so if he worked there for a certain number of years, almost all of his student loans would be forgiven.

It was just an added bonus that he, then Gail, fell in love with the town and the townspeople. They had already made plans, even before the wedding, to someday buy a small place outside of town so Gail could have her horse with her.

Gail asked Brian if he would let her leave her horse, Summer, at his farm when they married. Brian readily agreed, of course. What was one more mouth to feed, but what were friends for, anyway? They all laughed. The horses liked each other, so there was no problem there.

Beth would ride both Star and Summer, alternately, to keep them in shape.

Chapter 30

So, at the end of Beth's fifth year at the library, Gail and Matthew married. The wedding took place on Saturday afternoon. The happy couple left for their honeymoon to St. Marie Island, a secret dream of Gail for years. She had not even shared that with Beth, but told Matthew when he asked her where she wanted to go.

Beth, Brian, and Kelly were in their usual place on Brian's porch, about the usual time of the day. There was a spectacular sunset this evening. That, along with a gentle breeze blowing through the oak, providing a perfect coolness, made this the perfect ending to this day.

It was to become even more perfect, which might seem to be a contradiction in terms, but that's how Beth would remember it.

Kelly spoke first, as she often did. Beth had noticed that. Brian was the quiet one, but that complimented Kelly's more talkative, outgoing nature. Kelly had the tendency to make decisions quicker than Brian, who needed time to think things over and make a more deliberate decision. But, still, they had developed a compromise that worked.

"We wanted to wait until Beth and Matthew were married, of course, so there would be no questions that we would steal their thunder, so to speak, but Brian and I have decided to get married."

They were both watching Beth's face as Kelly made the announcement in quite a confident, serious way.

"It's about time," Beth said very nonchalantly, as if it were a routine announcement.

They didn't know what to make of it.

Then a slow smile began on her face that quickly became her full smile, her beautiful smile that everyone loved her for. She laughed as the other two joined in.

"I suppose you waited this long because of Number Three," she said, looking at Brian.

It had become a joke between the friends, now including Gail and Matthew. When everyone else seemed to know what was going to happen, what decision would be made out of seemingly endless discussions, they blamed it on Brian. He accepted this very well but knew his nature would not change. He just had to be sure he was doing the right thing.

The friends had talked among themselves, including with Kelly and they all knew this decision was coming. It was just a matter of time.

Brian's time.

And Kelly gave him that time. Love was there, no matter when.

"You have everything planned, of course," she said.

Kelly, as usual, answered her. "Of course. We wanted everything in place before we told anyone. Gail and Matthew will find out when they return in two weeks. But we haven't made the final reservations yet as to where we want to go, for a weekend only. We do know we want to marry in Wichita on a Saturday morning." She sighed. "I haven't told anyone this, it's just a dream, I guess, but I wish we could drive away from our ceremony in a fancy, jazzy sports car. I really can't picture us in the Honda or on the top of the John Deere tractor. Our wedding should be more special than that. But that's life. You go with the cards you're dealt. And being with Brian more than makes up for any car."

She reached out and took Brian's hand.

"But you do have a sports car, although it's a used one, not new, if you want it, that is, but with two conditions," Beth began.

Brian suddenly realized what she was talking about. "You mean the—"

"Yes, I will give it to you both, as my wedding gift to you, but with the two conditions I mentioned."

Brian had sat up and leaned forward toward her. "And what are those?" he asked.

Kelly was looking back and forth between them. She had no idea what they were talking about, but she didn't interrupt. She realized this was too important for that.

"You have to repaint it, and not red. You know cops see and watch a red sports car before any other vehicle. Dale can do his usual excellent work, and probably tell us what the most popular color in the country is, to blend in. You know, I still need it to 'hide in plain sight,' as it were. The other condition is that you somehow manage to change the VIN. I know autos can be tracked by that, which is unique to every vehicle. Think you can handle those two things? If not, I have to withdraw my offer, and you know why."

Brian hesitated.

Kelly saw her opportunity to jump into the conversation. She held up her hand. "Okay, stop, time out," she began. She put her right hand on top of her index finger of her left hand in the usual time-out signal. "I'm lost. I have no idea what you two are talking about. What *are* you talking about?"

Beth and Brian looked at each other.

"Come with us," Brian said. "Okay?"

He looked at Beth. He needed her permission to show Kelly, since she did bring it up.

Beth nodded her consent.

They walked down the steps off the porch and to the front of the barn.

"I'll get the keys," Beth said.

She opened one of the large double main doors of the barn just enough to get her body through and disappeared. A few seconds later she returned with two sets of keys in her hands.

First, they walked to the left to another set of double doors, but ones much smaller than those belonging to the main barn area. Kelly had seen this side part of the barn with the padlock on it. She just assumed it must house some old, antique piece of farm equipment, an old tractor or combine, maybe, from the days of Brian's grandfather.

Brian opened the padlock and removed it. He took one door, and Beth took the other. They walked backward, each opening the opposite way.

Inside was some sort of vehicle, but under a tarp.

Whatever it is, it must be valuable, Kelly thought.

Brian and Beth each took a side of the tarp and started rolling it backward, toward the interior of the garage, revealing the front end of a vehicle.

Kelly's eyes grew larger and larger as she saw more and more of what was being revealed. She couldn't believe her eyes when the whole tarp came off. "Wow!" she exclaimed. "Wow! I can't believe this." She started walking around the car, gently touching it. "This is a Camaro SS Turbo! What year? 2008? 2009? What?"

She was so excited.

"It's a 2010," Beth answered.

"Brian, you didn't tell me you had this."

"I don't. It isn't mine, and it wasn't mine to tell about," Brian answered.

Kelly stopped and looked at Beth.

"Yours?" she asked.

"You seem surprised. Can't a young lady own a car like this?"

"Well, yes, of course, I've always wanted one, it's just that…" She didn't finish her answer.

Beth laughed. Her beautiful laugh. "Just what?"

"I just didn't expect something like this, that's all. And you said you would give it to us, to Brian, or what? How can you just give something like this away? This is a very expensive car, even now. Did you buy it new, or what?"

She was so excited and full of questions.

"It was a gift for my high school graduation," Beth answered simply. She said it in such a way that indicated she didn't need any more questions about it.

Kelly knew her well enough by now that she caught her tone. She was surprised again. "But you seem to be older than—that would only make you…" Again, she couldn't finish.

"Are you saying I look old?" Beth asked, but in a teasing voice.

Kelly looked devastated. "No, of course not, but not…what…twenty-two? Twenty-three? You just seem older than that, I guess, more mature than someone your age."

Beth felt sorry for her. She was trying to get out of her statement. She laughed at her. "I'm just an old soul, I guess," she began. She looked at Brian. "The first condition, I know, is easy. Dale can do a super paint job. Can you think of something for the other? A different VIN? How can we manage that? It would be so much better for you guys to have the car than for it to just keep sitting here."

Kelly was still going around and around the car, stroking it. She still couldn't believe it. The fact that it could still be traced had not set in yet.

"I have an idea," Brian began, "but I need time to carry it through, to check to see if it can even be done."

"Do you want to tell me about it?" Beth asked.

"Not until I plan it all," he said, "but I'm sure it can be done the way I'm thinking of. With a lot of luck, that is. In the meantime, let's see if Dale can get it painted. We can drive it to the shop one evening when the license won't be so readable. I'll call him, but I know he'll love working on this baby!"

Dale was super excited when he heard what he had to work with. He would be able to cover the original canary yellow very well, even in obscure places. He promised no one would know it had been repainted.

When the three parted after the weekend, Brian said he might have a solution within a week, but it might take that long. Just not to worry.

Chapter 31

The first thing Brian did when Beth and Kelly left the farm, was to take the VIN tag off the inside dash of the Camaro. The original was put on with rosette rivets, he knew that, but he had the tool to take them off. He would take this tag with him.

The second thing was to locate the hidden VIN, which he found behind the firewall, and scratch through three of the numbers so they could not be read. If anyone ever had a reason to read this number, let him wonder about it. Brian could certainly claim innocence.

As soon as Beth said one of the conditions of giving them the car was that the VIN somehow be changed, Brian had thought of something he had not thought of for nine years. He kept in touch with an old high school buddy that he had taken a road trip with during the summer after they graduated, but he had forgotten some parts of the trip until something clicked when Beth mentioned the VIN.

They had driven everywhere that summer, sometimes to places they thought of on the spur of the moment. One of those places was through Oklahoma.

Once out of Kansas, they had dropped down on Interstate 35 and then went east to Tulsa. At first they headed out of Tulsa, south on the Broken Arrow Expressway, which would automatically become the Muskogee Turnpike, taking them farther south.

Just out of Broken Arrow, they decided they didn't want to stay on an interstate, which was not fun. They needed to see the countryside.

They exited off the turnpike toward Wagoner on State Highway 51. They knew better than to speed through any little town or community. There were "speed traps" in Kansas, the numerous little towns that stopped unsuspecting motorists for going a few miles over the speed limit. Therefore, as soon as the driver, either Brian or his friend, saw a speed limit sign, by the time they were at it, they were about five miles under the given speed.

In one little town, they went through at five miles under the 25 MPH posted on the west edge of the town. They laughed when they were back at the regular 60 MPH for the highway, because there had been a town police officer parked on the east side of a café, which a driver did not see until they were even with it. Had Brian been speeding, he would have been issued a ticket, for sure. It was the way these officers in these little towns made their own salary.

The way the two of them figured it, the cost of a ticket, not to mention it going on their driving record, was about equivalent to three, maybe four tanks of gas, and that took them farther on their trip, enabled them to enjoy more. They both knew they would never have another summer like this, so they wanted to make the most of it.

Giving money away wasn't part of the plan.

Brian only now understood why they decided to take the little state highway east into Arkansas, where the map showed they could drop down again to Interstate 40, if they wanted to.

Because on that country highway, around one curve they had to slow down for, they saw a big sign on the right that proclaimed "Jim White's Salvage" on a big sign. As soon as Brian saw it, he slowed down considerably. He glanced in his rearview mirror and saw that no one was coming behind him.

"Wow, look at that," his friend said. "I don't think I've ever seen such an old, or as large, a junkyard as this one. Look as those weeds. Some of those vehicles must have been here for more years than we can imagine. But look, along the front, there are some later model vehicles, also. You could almost think this place was a true grave-yard except for those."

"Oh, no," Brian returned. "That driveway is well used. But I thought all junkyards like this had to have a solid 'concealment' fence around them. Do you suppose Oklahoma doesn't have that law?"

"I've no idea, but this guy certainly doesn't obey that law. This is a real eyesore. But look, we're out in the middle of nowhere, so who do you think there is who cares if there's a fence keeping all this stuff out of view, or not? Besides, a fence around all this would cost tens of thousands of dollars. This guy doesn't have that kind of money, law or not."

"Don't you ever believe that," Brian said. "With a junkyard of this size, the owner here is probably a millionaire, selling all sorts of parts and items. He probably has every vehicle in there inventoried, with a list of parts. I understand nowadays these guys are even online, so you can reserve the part you need. It's a very sophisticated setup now."

"Really, I didn't know that," his friend said.

They were past the place by now, but it had impressed both of them, if for no other reason than its sheer volume of vehicles.

This was the place Brian remembered now. He even remembered the name. He looked online, but it was not there. So, the guy probably didn't report anything, either, and that was what Brian was counting on.

You see, Brian had worked most summers, except for the one at graduation, for Dale at his shop. Most of the time he had worked on the mechanic side. Dale had three large mechanic bays and two for body work, which were completely closed off from the mechanic side. It wouldn't do to get dust or anything on those expensive, custom paint jobs while they were drying.

Dale always said the devil was in the details.

Having worked there, and subsequently on the farm equipment with his dad when he was alive, and now on his own at the farm, Brian knew there was a federal law—the National Motor Vehicle Title Information system—that mandated that salvage yards report the VIN of salvaged vehicles, especially, he supposed, from insurance companies, for cars that had been declared "totaled" by them. This law was put into effect to prevent VIN fraud.

Dale had done the body work on numerous salvaged cars, which were only allowed to have the required liability insurance on them after the wreck they were probably involved in. But many people could only afford these salvaged, repaired vehicles, and Dale always did as good a job on these as any other. He felt the person deserved that.

Although thirty-seven states were trying to comply with this VIN reporting law, Brian hoped there were still some "good ole boys" out there who had owned and operated their "junkyards" for many years who thought they didn't have to do anything with this law. There was always someone, and he hoped to find that someone.

Some cities and locations had discontinued printing "white" and "yellow" pages. These numbers were all online now. Sure enough, Brian found "Jim White's Salvage" listed out of Tahlequah, which meant the telephone area covered a wide physical range.

He called the salvage yard.

"Jim White here. What can I do you for?"

"Mr. White, I'm glad I caught you. Would you, by any chance, have a wrecked 2010 Chevy Camaro SS turbo on your lot? I really need to locate one."

"Sorry, I don't have one of those. Will a Cobalt do?"

"No, sir," Brian responded. "I need the clutch from a Camaro. There's a slight difference between the two. The other wouldn't fit."

"You're right about that," White answered. "But some parts are compatible, so I thought I would ask."

"Mr. White, would you take my name and number and let me know if you get one in or if you can find one?" Brian asked. "I'm going to try to locate one in the meantime."

Mr. White took his name and number, but said he couldn't promise anything, of course.

Brian sat still after they hung up. He had been so sure that he would find a 2010 Camaro at that place. It just *felt* right. *Oh, well*, he thought. *I guess I'll start checking every town between here and Timbuktu.*

He found his paper atlas and started dialing. He had no luck the rest of the day. Several places assured him that they had never had one. The next morning, he started calling again. He had figured out a plan that went in a circle from Evansville, hoping to locate one as near to home as he could to eliminate travel time.

He stopped to eat the sandwich Sam had prepared for his lunch. He took the sandwich and a glass of sweet tea out to the back porch. He had hoped to surprise Beth with some good news, but he was starting to feel he would have to disappoint them all.

The sandwich finished, he had just taken his last swig of tea when his phone rang. The number looked vaguely familiar, but he couldn't place it immediately.

"Hello? Brian Greene here," he answered.

"Mr. Greene, this is Jim White, from the salvage yard here near Tahlequah. You called two days again looking for a 2010 Camaro SS Turbo. Do you still need the clutch from one?"

What is this? Brian thought. *I can't believe it.* "Yes," he said cautiously.

"Well, I have the car now," Jim said. "I think it's strange that I was able to buy the same Camaro you needed just after you called, but there it is. I'm looking at it right now. The next morning, after you called, an insurance company in Tahlequah called me. There had been an accident, and they had totaled this car. They asked me if I wanted to come and look at it, see if I wanted to buy it from them. I've bought several cars off them before. Said they thought of me first. I went right over there and bought it on sight. I could see the clutch assembly was intact, plus several other parts I could sell. I would certainly make money on the deal, so here it is."

"I can be there before noon tomorrow, if you will hold the clutch for me. I promise I'll be there," Brian said.

"I sure will. I still think it's a strange coincidence, don't you? You called about it, and here it is, like you conjured it up, or something," White said.

No, it's not a coincidence, Brian thought. *Just meant to be.* But, of course, he didn't say that to Jim White. He didn't tell Mr. White that his was the first place he had called.

He wouldn't have believed it, anyway. If you didn't believe in *The Force*, you just didn't.

"It was in a terrible wreck, the young mother and her daughter were killed. Mind you, it doesn't bother me to get a vehicle in here that's been in an accident, the insurance companies call me all the time, and if I can afford it, and see its parts value after I look at it, I buy it, but I hate it when someone has been killed, and it's coming to me to make money off it. You know what I mean?"

"I do, sir," Brian replied. He imagined how that could feel.

"You'll be the first person to get a part off her. That's good luck. By the way, I won't be here tomorrow, have some personal business to take care of, but my helper, a man named Carey, will be here. He's been with me for several years, so he can help you with anything. I'll leave him a note that you want the clutch, so he won't sell it to anyone else, if anyone else happens to come by."

Brian went to the barn to get his toolbox. He left as soon as he could. This was just after noon. He could make it to Tulsa by this evening.

He spent the night at the Hampton Inn, just off the Broken Arrow Expressway. He could eat a convenient breakfast there and be on his way in plenty of time. After walking to the nearby Cracker Barrel for dinner, he slept very well.

He was surprised how well he remembered how to get to the salvage yard. Here was the same small town he knew to go slowly through. There was what looked like the same police car waiting to catch someone speeding.

Then he was there.

Carey greeted him when he got out of his pickup. He glanced down at his toolbox, admiring it. Brian had been taught the value of a good toolbox and tools. He also brought his car jack with him. The owner might have had one he could use to jack up the vehicle, but Brian wasn't taking any chances. When Carey saw the jack, he nodded. At least the man must know what he was doing. You couldn't remove a clutch without jacking up the vehicle. Carey took him to the Camaro. Brian thought he was in danger of having Carey stand there, talking, but fortunately, another customer pulled up the drive just then.

Carey left, telling Brian to yell at him if he needed any help.

Brian said he would.

What further luck! This Camaro was also Canary Yellow, only the most popular color it came in. He had been hoping for that, also.

Brian immediately exchanged the VIN plate on the dash. He put the one from Beth's Camaro back on with rosette rivets, not the original rosette rivets, but he doubted if anyone would notice. At least he hoped not. Although, these guys might be savvier than he bargained for.

He had the tool. He smiled when he thought of his dad one time. His dad had to buy the tool for one time. He had complained that he probably would never have to use the damned tool another single time in his life.

His dad didn't.

To remove the clutch, first Brian unhooked the clutch cable and the positive battery cable. He had to separate the transaxle from the engine. He removed the bolts from around the flywheel bell housing and gently pushed the transaxle away from the engine. He had to expose the pressure plate.

He thought at first the transaxle was not going to budge, but with an extra groan and grunt on his part, it did. He put the transaxle back in place.

He had just finished when Carey returned, asking if he needed help. He apologized for having been gone, but he had a steady stream of customers coming and going all day.

"Hey, that's what you're here for, right? That's your bread and butter," Brian smiled.

"Jim will really be pleased, that's for sure," Carey said.

Brian took the clutch in the box Carey had provided, to his pickup and put it in the front seat. This was valuable. Nothing was going to happen to it if he could help it.

He went to the office with Carey, paid the stated amount, and took his receipt.

What Carey didn't know was that Brian had also scratched off several numbers on the hidden VIN, which he found behind the same firewall as Beth's. He had memorized Beth's VIN on the way here, so he knew which numbers to obliterate. This might well be attributed to the accident.

No one would ever know what happened.

If they even looked.

And it was unlikely that Jim White would report the VIN anyway, being as old school as he was. As Brian was happy to notice, there was still no "concealment" fence around the salvage yard.

෴

Carey was busy with customers to the end of the day, plus a little over. Tomorrow he was leaving to go on vacation to Florida, so he quickly put the money in the safe and the pile of receipts under the paperweight on the desk. Jim would find them in the morning.

The next morning, Jim was late getting to the salvage yard. He barely had time to count the money brought in yesterday and reconcile the amount to the invoices before the first customers came.

The Camaro proved to be a best seller, and many other parts besides the clutch came off of it. Reporting the VIN to the authorities was the last thing on Jim's mind. He didn't have time for such foolish laws anyway.

Chapter 32

Brian returned to Tulsa for the night, and then drove home the next day. It was still light outside, so he took the time to put the new VIN tag back on the Camaro. He took the tool, walked to the back of the barn, and then placed the tool under old tools in an old toolbox. This was his dad's old toolbox. These tools had not been used for years.

He called Dale, who told him to bring the Camaro to the shop that evening, after dark. He would start on it in the morning. Not only was Dale going to repaint the vehicle, but he did a thorough check-up, tune up, new tires, what he called "the works." Beth had authorized everything. She wanted to pay for it as her wedding gift to Brian and Kelly.

Brian's next call when Dale drove him home was to

Gail. He explained to her what they wanted to do. She agreed to call Uncle Nelson.

eɔeɔ

The Camaro sat in Dale's garage for three days after it was painted. They wanted to give it plenty of time to dry and pass Dale's final inspection.

The next Monday morning, Brian was at the tag agency at the county seat first thing. Nelson watched for him and waited on Brian himself. Brian had to fill out all the proper forms for lost title registration and tag, but that didn't take very long. He had the proper description and VIN for the vehicle.

Nelson issued him a new registration form, a new license plate, and current decal to put on the plate. Nothing came up with a red flag on the VIN. It was a good one.

The Camaro was now legally registered and tagged in the name of Brian Greene.

Chapter 33

Brian invited the friends to come to lunch at the farm on the following Saturday. Because of business, Kelly had not been there the weekend before, giving Brian plenty of time to work out his scheme.

Brian had said nothing to any of them, so they thought he was going to tell them he was unable to come up with a plan for the VIN. They were all ready to be disappointed. It was a good idea, but it just didn't happen for them.

Each one thought that, especially when they drove into the farm and saw the padlock back on the garage door on the side of the barn.

The Camaro was still in hiding!

Brian saw them coming and walked down the steps

to meet them. They all got there at the same time, which was amazing. It was almost as if it had been planned, but it was not.

As they climbed out of their vehicles, Brian motioned them over to the barn. The padlock was not locked.

After greetings and hugs all around, Brian said, "Come and stand over here." He pointed to a spot that would allow the double doors of the garage to open fully.

"Beth, this was your idea. Why don't you come and help me with these doors?"

They opened the doors as wide as they could. As they opened, they all saw a beautiful white Camaro sitting there.

"You did it!" Gail exclaimed.

Brian grinned. "Actually, Dale did it."

"Look! Look!" Beth said. She was the first to notice the new license with the current year's decal on it. "You did it. You got a new VIN. You did it!"

She started dancing around, hugging each of them. Her joy was infectious, and they all clapped and shouted.

"Thanks to you-know-who," Brian said over the noise.

"Uncle Nelson," Gail said immediately. "What a lifesaver he has been this second time."

"What do you mean, this second time?" Kelly asked. "And who is Uncle Nelson?"

They all laughed. Of course, she didn't know Beth's

story and Uncle Nelson's role in it. It was time to tell her. She was more than a trusted friend at this point. She was going to be part of the family, this wonderful family of best friends.

Before they went into the house for lunch and explanations, they all went around and around the car, admiring Dale's work. They looked at the new paperwork, courtesy of Uncle Nelson. Beth and Gail insisted that Brian and Kelly take the car for a spin while they prepared lunch. After all, they could legally drive it now.

Kelly could hardly wait. Brian tossed her the keys and off they went. The beautiful sound of the high-powered engine almost made Kelly cry. This was what she had always dreamed of. Of course, white would not have been her first choice, not for a car like this, but she knew she would hear the explanation for it.

And you didn't look a gift horse in the mouth. Her mother had taught her that.

She did hear Beth's story over lunch, only it was a condensed, edited version. She did not reveal her real name to her or the name of her hometown. She told enough to be acceptable to her—a story of having to leave home at eighteen, coming to stay with Gail, who she had met at summer camp.

No lies, just not all the truth.

Gail and Brian remained quiet. They let Beth tell just what she wanted to. It was her story and her life. She simply said Uncle Nelson helped her with a new driver's license under another name.

It was enough and, most importantly, believable. Kelly was amazed but knew when she first met her that Beth was special. And strong. How strong she had to be to drive away from her home like that at that age. She knew her well enough by now not to ask what her former, probably her birth, name was. She also realized she was being trusted with information that would remain secret. She would never tell.

She would always be Beth Conners to her. Beth with the big heart and beautiful smile.

They all agreed they were glad she was here now.

This was at the end of her fifth year of living here.

Chapter 34

The wedding was planned. Beth met Brian and Kelly at a five-star restaurant in Wichita. This was a pre-wedding celebration just for the three of them. After lunch, they had two hours before the wedding, which was to take place at the Wichita City Hall. Gail and her husband, Matthew, would be there, as well as Kia, her husband, Steven, and Grandma Susan. A few of Brian and Kelly's good friends would also attend. They didn't need anything fancy, just the company of good friends they chose.

Yes, Kia had married while still at the university. Beth didn't know who continued to pay for the tuition. She didn't ask. Maybe Kia's husband, Steven, had the funds.

As they rose from their table to leave the restaurant, Brian made a funny remark, and Beth's laughter rang out across the room.

Chapter 35

Clayton's head jerked up.

It couldn't be! But it had to be! There could not be two laughs like that in the whole world.

Misee Sue's laugh, it had to be!

At the same split-second he heard the laughter and had those thoughts, he spun around. He saw a beautiful young lady with short dark hair and glasses, standing at a table across the room, laughing with a young couple she was with. They were gathering their personal items to leave.

At that instant, she glanced his way, and their eyes met. Did hers open wide, or did he imagine it, wanting recognition to be there?

Misee Sue! It *was* Misee Sue, he knew it was! She had changed her looks, but he recognized her. After all, he had looked at that beautiful face for years and years.

Also in the same second, his long legs started carrying him across the room. The young couple was gone. Halfway across the room, he called, "Misee Sue! Misee Sue!"

He thought he saw the slightest hesitation in her shoulders, but maybe he only wanted it to be there.

She was walking away, in the opposite direction. He caught up with her. He touched her shoulder. He dropped his hand when she stopped.

"Please, Misee Sue, don't pretend you didn't hear me call your name and don't pretend that you didn't see it was me. Please don't pretend right now that you don't know me. Please!"

Yes, she had recognized him when she happened to look that way as Brian and Kelly turned away. She had quickly looked down and just as quickly grabbed her bag. She needed to get away before he recognized her, but she was afraid he had.

They both had blinked in that second. The recognition was there.

Now, she almost decided to pretend she didn't know him, that he had mistaken her for someone else, and please excuse her—but something, *something*, made her change her mind. How the brain could think that fast was a mystery.

She looked up at him. "Okay, Clay, I won't pretend that I didn't hear you call my name, or that you didn't just touch my shoulder, or that you didn't recognize me. It's me, and it's you. Happy?"

She started to turn away from him again.

He reached out and grabbed her by the upper arm.

She turned toward him, very startled, looked down at his hand on her arm, and up at him. She raised her eyebrows.

He very quickly let go of her arm. "I'm sorry, I'm so sorry that I grabbed your arm that way. Please forgive me for doing that. I know I've never done that to you, but you were turning away, and I can't stand to lose you for a second time in my life, I really can't. Don't turn away, Misee Sue, please don't. I've found you, and I couldn't stand the thought of losing you again."

"I didn't realize I'm lost," she responded in a cool, indifferent tone. "A person can't find something that isn't lost."

Oh, God, I'm losing her, or I've lost her, or whatever. Please don't say it's true, please, don't let it happen! He realized he was praying, silently, but still praying.

She wasn't sure of what she just said. Was she rambling? When she looked up and across the room and saw Clayton looking at her, her heart had literally flopped in her chest. She had heard about that happening with people, but really didn't believe it happened. Her heart had also started beating faster, which she also thought would never happen again. And with the man who had always made it beat faster when they were teenagers.

True, she had allowed herself to think of him briefly, but ever so briefly, during the last five years. But it had never been with the affection and love she felt for him when they were eighteen and made such wonderful plans for their lives together. But there had always been such a feeling of indifference that immediately set in, hardening her heart and thoughts.

After all, he *had* been the first to turn away. The thought of that action with the look in his eyes right before he turned away, during that first evening into the night that she sat on the baseball field had been the beginning of her indifference, the beginning of a time of experiencing no feeling at all when she thought of him, then no feelings for anyone else during that next week had hardened her heart. Those six days of Hell. If there was a Hell on earth, she had gone through it then. Thus, her decision to leave. Beginning with Clay's rejection of her. And, now, here he was, standing in front of her, looking as handsome—no, as beautiful—as ever. If a man could be beautiful, he always had been. Even now women who walked past them turned to look at him, admiring him. She saw that.

How was she supposed to act, or react, whichever. She decided to act. "Nice to see you again, Clayton," she began. "I really must go now. Enjoy your day."

She used her best professional voice, firm but kind. It always let a person know the conversation was over. She turned away for the third time.

"No, I beg you, Misee Sue, please don't go. Let me explain, let me talk to you about everything. Please!"

Something in the tone of his voice made her turn back, again, for the third time.

There was a forlorn, almost pitiful tone in that strong, baritone voice of his. She had never heard this Clayton before. She had certainly never heard him beg before, for anything, at any time, and later she would admit that's what made her turn around to face him.

That was the turning point. The third time was the charm.

But she wasn't ready to accept him back into her life, as he found out.

"Please, may we sit somewhere, have some coffee or something, and talk? Do you really have to be somewhere, or did you just say that?"

"Yes, I do," she responded, looking down at her watch, "in exactly one hour and forty-five minutes now, and I won't be late. In fact, I will be early. The two people you just saw me with are getting married. They are best friends of mine, and I won't miss the ceremony for the world."

"Fine, we'll get you there. Where?" he asked, as they walked to a café with tables and chairs out front.

They sat down. A barista immediately came to them and took their order for coffee. He realized they didn't even see him. He thought that maybe he would find someone like that to love, someday. They obviously loved each other very much.

"City hall," she answered.

He smiled. "That's very close. We have no worries."

She felt her heart melt inside her and that made her afraid. That was the feeling that came to her—fear. Why she should be afraid of Clayton, she could not explain just then, maybe never.

After their coffee came, he started to explain about the game, but just like she did with Kia that time, she held up her hand for him to stop. "I don't want to hear anything about it, and I do mean *anything*," she emphasized. "Nothing to do with our hometown or anything that happened there. That is not part of my life now, and that's how I want to keep it. If you want to talk about yourself, only, and what you've been doing for the past five years, then, fine, but nothing else. Understand? If you start, I will get up and walk away, and you won't follow me. I mean it, Clayton."

Again, he heard and felt the hardness of her voice, saw the steel in her eyes. He knew he had to back off, and he did. "Misee Sue, it has been five years, thirty-two weeks, and one day since I saw you last. There's so much I want—no, I need to tell you—"

"You're wrong, you know," she interrupted.

Clayton blinked. He looked blank for a second. "Wrong about what? What are you talking about?"

"It hasn't been five years, thirty-two weeks, and one

day since you saw me last. It's been five years, thirty-two weeks, and two days. You're wrong, that's all there is to it."

She couldn't believe he had been counting all this time. She had, of course, she had to admit that. But only she knew about it all this time, until right now, when she found herself confessing it to Clayton.

She had started the day of the ballgame, putting a big "X" on each day of a pocket-sized calendar just before she went to bed. That day was gone, a day without him. She kept it up all this time. Tonight would have been another "X," another day gone by without him. She foresaw a lifetime of little calendars piling up in her drawer.

But he had been counting. That had to mean that he also missed her.

Clayton had quickly recovered from his surprise when she said that. She had been counting, also? "So, where do you get the two days? I started the next morning after the game."

"Well, I started that evening, because that's when you left me. I had to count that day."

"But we had been together most of that day. That didn't count as a day without you."

"It ended without you, that's all I knew and still know. So, it's two days."

Clayton smiled. "I'm going to have to stay with the 'one,' or I'll get totally off from now on, I know I will. But maybe I won't have to count from now on. Do I?"

This last he asked softly. If he hoped for reassurance from her, he was disappointed.

Instead, she changed the subject by asking him to talk about himself for the last five years, give or take.

He told her about his university years, how he watched for her all the time, especially at the beginning of each semester, but she never showed. He felt that going to college had been so important to her that surely, eventually, she would show up. But she hadn't.

She didn't comment on anything, just listened.

After graduating, with a double major, those being in physical education and a teaching credential, he went back to Cedarville. Coach had a stroke, had to retire, and Clayton was lucky enough to get the position. He had to coach all the athletics, plus teach Social Studies. Their town hadn't changed that routine forever. He also accepted the position of teacher of the fifth and sixth grade boys for Sunday School, at the same church they had attended for years.

He shared with her that it made him get into a routine, though, and he needed that. He also hoped she would show up in town one day.

He looked up at her when he said that. She didn't respond.

She had given him her full attention the whole time, though, so he was grateful for that.

"And about Marie—" he started, before he remembered what she had said.

She reacted immediately. Her hand went up again. "No!" She looked at her watch. He had talked for over an hour, and it was time to go. She stood up, as he did. She would never know why she said what she said next. "Would you like to attend the wedding ceremony with me? Brian and Kelly won't mind."

Where did that come from? But he was answering. She couldn't get out of it now. Maybe he would decline.

No such luck. What was she doing?

"Are you sure? It's their wedding."

"If you come in with me, it'll be fine. They will wonder who you are, of course, but I'll explain," Beth urged.

Clayton went with Beth to the ceremony. When Brian, who was standing at the front of the room, saw her walk in with Clayton, he raised his eyebrows in question.

She just shrugged. The ceremony was about to begin, so they all took their places. Clayton sat out in the audience area, toward the back, while Beth walked up front to stand beside Brian. She didn't mind being best man for her best friend.

Brian and Kelly left to total well wishes. They were going to drive to their weekend destination, before their planned honeymoon in a couple of weeks. It would be a wonderful drive in the Camaro.

Beth said good-bye to Clayton outside city hall. He asked, but she would not give him her phone number. She asked him to write down his phone number and email. He quickly wrote it on a piece of paper she provided. She made him promise not to follow her when she walked away. He didn't, but he wanted to. He watched her walk the half block to the end of the building then turn the corner. He had a bad feeling that he would not see her again.

Meeting her like this, quite by chance, had been a blessing.

At least she had taken his phone number.

She would call.

Chapter 36

As Beth walked away, her heart was singing. She was happy, not only for the fact that she had just been with him, could have touched him, if she had allowed herself, but for the fact that he had actually counted the days, as she had.

Since he had given the time in years, weeks, and days, she did, also. She could easily have given the total amount of days, which she bet he could have, too. She surprised him when she admitted she had kept count of the time away from him.

But she was not ready to jump back into his arms. That's why she asked him not to follow her, not to know what kind of vehicle she drove. For this reason, she deliberately made a left turn at the corner, when her car was actually parked the opposite way, about two blocks down.

She decided to go back into city hall from the rear and exit out the front again. She would turn and make several other turns around blocks before she made it to her car. Hopefully, she wouldn't run into Clayton by doing that.

There had been too much hurt and humiliation, especially at the graduation ceremony, when no one had responded to the special hand signal of the class. Not even Clayton had responded. That's when she knew everyone was against her. How she had held out all week until that Friday, she could not imagine.

She was just thankful she was where she was right now.

She had lived in Evansville for over five years.

Chapter 37

Clayton finally had to admit to himself that Misee Sue was probably not going to call. He also admitted that he kept saying "probably." Every day that went by, he decided to give her just one more day, just one more day, to call. She would probably call tomorrow.

But it had been six months, exactly, to the day. This was the evening of the day that marked six months since they had seen each other across that restaurant. He had found her, again, but six months had gone by since she walked out of his life.

Again.

At the time, he had said all he could have said. At least he said all she allowed him to say. He didn't even tell her he loved her. He should have done. He knew that now. Maybe that would have made all the difference. Maybe she would have forgiven him for that fateful evening when he turned his back on her and walked away.

Why had he done that? Just why did he do that? He had asked himself that so many times, that he would have been a millionaire by now if someone had given him a penny for every time he asked it.

He sighed.

It was time to give up. Not really, he knew, but to get on with his life, somehow. He knew it would go on without Misee Sue, but it would never be the same.

He was sitting on his sofa with the TV on in front of him, but he did not hear a word of the program.

He decided to call a woman he had met, named Melissa. A new teacher had come last year, and Melissa was the teacher's sister, who had chanced to come to visit one weekend and go to a party that Clayton also attended. He was actually thinking that Misee Sue should be there with him when he was introduced to Melissa. He had to admit that she was a beautiful woman. She just wasn't Misee Sue. There would never be another like Misee Sue for him.

Later, his colleague told him that Melissa had really been impressed by him, why didn't he give her a call? She would be very receptive to it.

Why not call her? he thought. *I have to forget about Misee Sue and move on.*

He rose up from the sofa and was halfway to the

kitchen when his phone, which was on the counter, rang. "No, I don't want to go out for a drink," he said, out loud.

He assumed it was one of his buddies wanting to go to the local bar. It was really not Clayton's scene, though. They just all thought he was crazy, waiting around for who-knew-what. They all had thought for years that Misee Sue was dead. So, in their opinion, he needed to get out more. They called all the time, hoping he would come with them.

"Hello?" he said, his voice flat.

"It has now been six years, two weeks, and two days since you walked away," said a familiar voice.

"Misee Sue," he breathed. "It's you!"

"Yes, it's me, are you still available? I mean, are you seeing someone special by now? I know it's been six months, and maybe you've given up on me, but—"

"I would never give up on you, and it's been six years, two weeks, and one day." He laughed. "You never could do math right."

Misee Sue laughed. A thrill went through him. That wonderful laugh of hers. He thought he would never hear it again.

"If you're free, would you like to meet somewhere, sometime?"

"Oh, of course, I would, you know that. You just say when and where, and I'll be there, no matter what. If I don't show up, you can figure I've had a car wreck or something, racing to you. Otherwise, nothing will keep me away."

They agreed on a place and time on the following Saturday. Kia had a special meeting, so Beth had the time. She had not missed her times with Kia and Grandma, nor missed a Saturday at work. Would she have met him on a Sunday? she wondered. Of course, she would have.

That was their new beginning. Clayton never questioned her about the six-month time span between their meeting in the restaurant and her phone call. He didn't feel he had the right to question any of her actions.

Their time was from now on, and that was all that mattered.

Chapter 38

At the end of her sixth year in Evansville, which meant it was at the end of the school year, the Evansville athletic coach resigned. He moved on to a much bigger town, which meant a much bigger school, which meant an advance in his coaching career. He was young and had grandiose plans. Someday he wanted to be the coach of a professional football team.

That left the position in Evansville open.

In a month, a young man named C.J. Wilkes appeared before the school board and was hired. This was a move up for him. He had taught for the past two years at a 1-A school, and this was 2-A, so he would have a little bigger challenge.

But he had gone to the finals with the other team, so Evansville had high hopes.

It didn't hurt that the young man could also teach Civics and a class of Senior English.

His photo appeared in the local newspaper, of course, and the town gave him a reception at a restaurant.

Brian was present.

Brian's marriage to Kelly had not created the stir or backlash in this small town that he thought it might. Even here, in Smalltown, USA, most people respected and accepted the lifestyle of another. Oh, there was the usual small group of self-righteous, judgmental types, but they were in any town, large or small. Besides, most people here liked Brian and then grew to love Kelly when they met her, person to person.

A few days after the reception, Beth was in her usual chair on his back porch when he returned home from grocery shopping. Yes, Sam still cooked for him and usually bought the groceries, but occasionally he wanted to buy special items.

He wasn't surprised to see her. She had been welcome there for many years, long before Kelly had moved there after the wedding. Kelly was gone on business at this particular time, although she usually worked from home. She had specialized in patent law, so her research could be done from anywhere, and she chose to do it from home. Her firm, though small by big-city standards, had contracts from several of the large firms around the country to research any patents presented to them by their big corporations.

It kept Kelly busy, but she loved it. She loved working at the farm.

At home.

Brian took the groceries into the kitchen and put away what needed to be. He fixed a glass of iced tea and joined Beth on the porch.

There sat in silence for a few minutes, then Brian spoke, "Let me ask you something."

Beth looked over at him, raising her eyebrows. He was used to this look.

"You can tell me it's none of my business, and tell me it isn't so, or anything you want to, but I hope you tell me the truth."

Now, her curiosity was really up.

"What is it?" she asked.

"This is something else, something I feel is important. Not to me, at least maybe not right now, maybe later, but important to you."

"You really have me curious. What is it?" She could not imagine what he was about to say.

He made a gesture in the air with his hand. "Okay, tell me I'm wrong, but isn't this young coach that's just been hired, this C.J. Wilkes, doesn't he look just like the young man you brought to our wedding two years ago?"

She didn't move. Her facial expression did not change. There was no surprise anywhere because of the question. But he recognized this response from her. He had seen it every once in a while through the years.

This look meant she might be shutting him out. There might not be a response to his question.

But she knew honesty was all she could give this best friend of hers. She looked over at him and smiled. "You have a good memory. Yes, he's the same man. Isn't it a coincidence that he's taken a position in this town?" She grinned.

He knew he was okay in having asked the question.

"Humph," he responded, in the best imitation of a grunt he could give. "We both know there are no coincidences in this world. All things happen for a reason, in their own place and time. How long have you two been dating?"

"Since we met in New York City."

"That long, huh?" he asked. "And I thought, at the time, that Kelly and I had become the experts at dating without anyone knowing. I think you two have done a better job."

"Thank you, I think, but may I tell you something, just between you, me, and the fence post?"

"Of course," he replied. He knew this meant not to repeat it. He wouldn't.

"C.J. is my high school sweetheart. I call him Clay. If you hear me call him that, although I'll always try not to, then just ignore it."

"Well, well, well," he said, quietly. "So, why say it's only been two years that you two have been dating? What was high school?"

"And what is that supposed to mean?" Beth asked him.

"Nothing. It's just interesting, that's all." He knew in this moment there was more to the story of her leaving home than he had been told…what…six…seven?…years ago, now.

"We will probably get married," she said simply.

"Oh, yeah?" Brian responded. "When is this happening?"

"Not yet, not for a while, maybe a long time, oh, I don't know…" she answered. She made a helpless gesture in the air.

He had never seen her flustered. He waited. He knew there was more to come.

"His real name is Clayton James Wilkeson. We agreed that he would change his name to apply for this position. That way, the people in our hometown would not recognize it, where he had gone to. In other words, if some old friend or relative knew he was here and came to visit, they might accidentally spot me. And that wouldn't do."

This man had something to do with Beth leaving home at eighteen, Brian thought.

Beth was continuing. "…I told you about leaving home, but not why, and thank you for never asking during all these years."

Brian dismissed that with a toss of his hand. It hadn't been his place to ask. He knew if she wanted to tell him anything, she would, and it seemed that right now she was going to tell him…well, something…maybe not all. But he would take whatever she wanted to reveal.

"I left that town, my—our, Clay's and mine—hometown, because everyone thought I told a lie about something very, very important. I didn't, but no one believed me. I was totally shunned, even by my own parents, for over a week. I was the valedictorian at my high school graduation—"

Yeah, she would have been, Brian thought.

"—and the class gave no response to me, even ignored a special signal we had used, all of us, the whole class, since ninth grade. I walked out of the gym determined to leave the first chance I had, and that was the next Friday morning. But going back to the day of the so-called lie by me, at the time, the very time, Clay was the first person to turn away, to not believe me, or believe in me, if that's a better way to put it, to start shunning me."

Brian saw such a pained expression on her face, as she relived that memory that he wanted to reach out and take her hand. But he didn't. He stayed very still, not wanting to break the mood of this confession.

"We had known since third grade that we were meant for each other, that we were soul-mates. We had declared our love for each other, made plans to go to university together, and then marry, spend the rest of our lives together."

Again, several emotions crossed her face.

She looked at Brian and smiled.

"Did he ask you before he took this job, moved here, or did he just come?"

"Oh, no, we talked about it, and I agreed that he should put in his application and see what came of it. I told him we could start seeing each other occasionally, see where a relationship, if any, went from there. He's young. If nothing developed between us, he could always get a position somewhere else. I just need to give it time. I still hurt. I still feel the pain of the look on his face and in his eyes when he turned away. He's apologized so much already, but I need time. He knows this," she concluded.

She had finished saying all she was going to at this point, he could tell.

"I understand. I think…well, I knew how I felt about Kelly from the moment our eyes met in that deli, but I needed time and space, also, to be sure. Not only to be sure of her, but to be sure of myself, who I was, and who I wanted to spend my life with. So, yes, I understand how you feel about waiting and wanting to be sure of…Clay, is it?"

"I call him Clay. I've always been the only one to do that. I'll try to remember to call him C.J. around here, but if I don't, maybe people will just think it's a nickname. Getting back to you, I knew you would understand because of how you felt about Kelly and the time you took to be sure," she responded. "Again, this is between you, me, and the fencepost out there." She laughed and pointed to the corner of the paddock fence. The horses were at the rail, looking at them.

"How about the horses? I think they might have heard." Brian laughed with her. She was going to be all right.

Beth stood up, as Brian did as well.

"Let's go talk to them," she said, "I have to make them promise not to say anything."

They laughed and went to pat the horses.

Right now, Kelly was driving up the driveway.

"Mum's the word," Brian said, before Kelly got out of her car. "Until then, I wish you all the happiness in the world, you know that. Always."

"I know," she replied.

They greeted Kelly.

Chapter 39

The seventh year went by quickly.

A few days after Beth and Brian had their talk about C.J., Gail and Matthew announced they were going to have a baby. This would be their second child. They welcomed him at the usual time. He weighed seven pounds, ten ounces, and was twenty inches long. They named him Luke.

It seemed that Gail was holding true to her statement that she wanted Mark, Luke, and John, since she was married to a Matthew. It was a quaint idea, but she said, that way, maybe she would always be able to remember their names and who was the oldest, the next, and the youngest.

The obvious question was asked when Luke was born. What would the name be if they had a fourth boy?

Gail just laughed and said she would probably have a girl, but she would face that when it came!

The same city councilman who had contributed the patron checkout/check-in and online access system for the library came in one day. He found Miss Betty and Beth in the small area they used for Children's Story Time, and realized they didn't have the space they needed in this small library, because they were taking down a table and stacking extra chairs to take to the storeroom.

They started talking. He heard the two librarians' dreams of an area just for the Children's Library and showed him what they had sketched—several alternatives.

The library had extra land space on one side. It was a double-lot within the town. He wanted to help.

The man fussed at them. He said, didn't he tell them when the new computers went in to let him know if they needed anything else? He had just assumed for these few years that everything was okay, even though the small city had grown by several hundred people, and half of those were children. It just hadn't dawned on him that the library needed to grow with the city. In several months, the library was expanded. New furniture was bought for both the Children's Library and the library in general.

Six months into that year, Beth and C.J. were seen having dinner together and then going to other places together. The townspeople approved.

Of course, Miss Betty took credit for having introduced them. When C.J. first came as coach, during the past summer, he casually strolled into the library one day, just to check it out—he said, excuse the pun! Miss Betty was the first person he saw. She called to Beth to come to the front and introduced them. She swore at that exact moment, it was "love at first sight" for both of them.

From then on, through the years, she told that story over and over, because C.J. and Beth became town favorites.

During that first year as Coach, C.J. led the football team to the state championship, and now the baseball team was going to the finals. The school board members patted themselves on the back for the wise choice they made when they hired this young man. They also marveled at the fact that a young man his age wanted to live and work in such a small town. But they all agreed it must have been a "meant to be" thing because he and Beth fell in love.

Beth and C.J. announced their wedding plans, and everyone rejoiced. It would be a town event, of course, and at their church.

They were married at the end of this seventh year that Beth had lived in Evansville.

The townspeople agreed with each other, you just never knew when and where you were going to meet the one you would love and marry!

The names on the marriage license, obtained at the courthouse in the county seat, were Clayton James Wilkeson and Elizabeth Ann Connors.

Chapter 40

The baseball team won the state 2-A championship. C.J. sure knew his baseball! Everyone agreed on that.

Kia had her second child, a boy. He weighed eight pounds, two ounces and was twenty inches in length. Just an average, healthy baby. They named him Jackson. Kia had wanted to name him Latimer, but her husband, Steven, wasn't sold on the idea. She wanted to explain to him why she wanted that name, but knew she couldn't. It would have opened a "can of worms," and she kept her promise to Misee Sue—uh—Beth. Kia would always think of her as Misee Sue, and she had to watch through the years that she called her sister, Beth.

Steven had met Beth, of course, but she was introduced as a friend Kia had met during her first year of college, while Beth was visiting another friend there. Steven thought no more about it but enjoyed being with Beth and C.J. when they were together.

Kia breathed a sigh of relief. From that time on, she was more careful. C.J. had agreed early on that Kia was a good friend. That wasn't a lie, as he considered that she was. Everyone assumed Beth was, also.

Kia, Grandma, and Beth continued their Saturday meetings. Steven knew the special bond they had and didn't worry about it. Those Saturdays he could catch up on projects around the house and the never-ending "honey-do" list. He enjoyed it. He watched the children on those days, also. Sometimes he had more patience with them than Kia did.

Chapter 41

The years went on, as years do.

Gail did have another son, and they named him John, as planned, since he was a boy. They decided that three children was enough.

Beth and C.J. had two children, first a girl, who weighed six pounds, four ounces and was twenty-one inches long, a tiny bundle of joy, with blonde hair and blue eyes. Since Beth had dark hair, everyone said she must take after C.J., who had lighter hair and hazel eyes. They named her Susan, after Beth's grandmother.

Beth and Kia had talked about this. Beth asked if Kia had a girl first, did she want to name her after Grandma? Kia said, no, why didn't Beth take that name, since Grandma never wavered or doubted that Beth had told the truth. That would honor their grandma, who, indeed, was pleased that little Susan was named after her.

Their second child was a boy, a whopping eight pounds, thirteen, ounces, and twenty-one inches in length. They named him Jason, for no particular reason except that they liked the name.

Brian and Kelly loved the children, especially the girls, Susan and Abigail, Kia's first child. One day at a cookout with everyone, Brian and Kelly announced that they had decided to adopt a little girl. They had already started the paperwork.

Little Jessica came to them when she was only three days old and was welcomed into the fold.

Everyone was very happy, of course. There would be another family member to love. And they all considered themselves family, although they had all started out being friends. There was never the concept of a "godparent," as such, because their belief did not have that designation, but they talked and knew that each of the children, later grandchildren, would always be taken care of by someone.

Sure, there were aunts and uncles among the parents, of course, but they were growing older along with everyone else.

As a family, as the children grew, Beth and C.J. decided to support the American Association of Independent Professional Baseball. There were ten teams, and they played at cities nearer Kansas than the major professional teams. The families bought season passes and traveled as a group with other supporters to the games. The Wichita Wingnuts were their favorite, but that was from the home state. You had to have them as the favorite.

Of course, the families went to the high school games, since Dad was coach. How could they not? The football and basketball teams always went to semi-finals, if not finals themselves. They won most of the games they played.

All the children learned the song "Take Me out to the Ball Game" when they were young, and they had to sing it during every trip. The first time it was sung to them, by Beth and C.J., Jason wanted to know what "Cracker Jack" was. It became a favorite candy of them all. Not only did they always have to sing the song, they had to stop at the nearest Dollar General Store to load up on Cracker Jack for the journey to and from a ballgame.

Kia and her family, being farther away, attended the games when they could.

C.J.'s parents came when they could, although travel was difficult for both of them. They had been "older" parents when they had C.J., so they were "getting up there." They had not been able to attend the wedding of C.J. and Beth, so tried to make up for it. Everyone assured them it was okay, just come when they could.

All the children grew up playing sports. Baseball quickly became the favorite in the Wilkes family, with Susan becoming an excellent player.

One time, when the children were in elementary school, at a community picnic, two teams formed to play a sandlot game.

Beth was chosen for one of the teams, but the team, comprised mostly of men, did not expect much of her. After all, they were just playing for fun.

C.J. knew what to expect from Beth, but no one else did.

To everyone's surprise, when she stepped up to home plate, she had the correct stance, held the bat correctly, her arms in the proper position to bat.

The first pitch was a ball. The second pitch, however, came in hard and straight.

With a sound that carried throughout the park, Beth hit the ball so hard, it soared low and long, far beyond the fielders, who had moved in when she came to the plate.

To their further surprise, Beth ran so fast around the bases, she made it to home almost before the ball hit the ground, a long way behind the fielders. In fact, as she ran the bases, everyone started shouting at the other two to hurry up or Beth was going to catch them.

She had batted in two other runners and there was only one out. Everyone was amazed and congratulated her. Beth and C.J. exchanged a knowing glance and grin.

In the years to come, Beth was always the first to be chosen, even fought over, when teams formed. Susan and Jason were always proud of her. Beth never made an issue of being a good baseball player. She just always did her best.

The joke was, though, she just could never do better than C.J. There was never any pressure on the children, though, only to do their best, which never had to be anyone else's best. This held true in their school work, also. Any competition was healthy and fun, never competitive enough to stress anyone.

Chapter 42

Jason was not an athlete. He admitted that to himself after a couple of years of T-ball and Little League. When it came time to form a team for the coming year, the family talked about it. Everyone was excited.

Everyone except one.

Beth and C.J. had talked about Jason several times. They knew he did not enjoy athletics, especially baseball. It seemed he was always the last batter when his team had two outs. All the players and fans in the stands knew he was going to strike out, providing the third out and usually the losing out. You could hear a collective moan when he came to bat. He heard it, too, but always played "for the Gipper."

This year, C.J. turned to him and said, "Jason, you really do not want to play ball, especially baseball, do you?"

Poor Jason's eyes went wide. He was afraid to say anything, afraid they would be so disappointed in him, even Susan, and this he could not bear.

"It's all right," Beth said. "You don't have to, if you don't want to."

Jason looked at his dad. Could this be right? What would his dad say?

"I agree, you don't have to, if you don't want to," C.J. responded.

They saw an actual physical sigh take place within Jason. It felt, to everyone, like the weight of the world came off his shoulders.

"Really?" he asked. "I really don't want to. I don't like to, and I know I can't play. I know I always make the last out and everyone hates me."

"No one hates you," C.J. said. "Some people just have more athletic ability than others, or none at all, and now you won't have to worry about it. But what would you like to do? There must be something you are interested in."

"Well, if you really want to know, I really would like to play the trombone. Mr. Peabody, the music teacher at school last year, had me try one, and I really liked it. Oh, I know it would take a lot of practice and you would probably want to run me out of the house at first, but a person has to start somewhere, right?"

He gave his special grin that the parents always responded to.

"You're right," Beth said. "If Mr. Peabody is willing to give you private lessons, as well as with the band at school, we will certainly support you. We just ask that, if you start this, you make a commitment to follow up on it, at least to the point that you know if you are good or bad and want to do something with your music for your life. If, after several years, you know it will only be a hobby for life, we can talk about other things, then. How does that sound?"

It sounded great to Jason. He showed immediate improvement and a continued interest in the instrument. Beth and C.J. wondered where the musical ability came from, and then C.J. remembered that his paternal grandfather could play anything and sing anything he wanted to. He just never had the opportunity to do anything with his music. In that time, he had to work and provide for his family.

Fortunately for Jason, this small town had a major interest in the arts in school, not just music, but its art program. This was thanks to a trust fund set up for that purpose by a benefactor. Jason flourished under the one-on-one training of his teacher, who later recommended someone that could carry Jason further.

Jason flourished both musically and academically, although his patience did not at times. He set himself almost unreachable goals at a young age.

It was suggested that Jason apply to the University of the South in Sewanee, Tennessee, which was forty miles north of Chattanooga, for their summer music camp. This was at age ten. Even at that age, he was required to fill out an application almost on the college level. He had to have recommendations from music educators. Also, the parents had an oral interview over the phone.

This program was five weeks long. Children were accepted from all over the country, ranging from ages seven to high school age. All of them had one thing in common—music!

Beth and C.J. packed the car with all the things Jason might need for five weeks. Little room remained for the family, but they all piled in. It was a long drive for them, but it was rewarding. None of them had been in this part of the country or experienced the Southern culture.

Sewanee was amazing. It was built like a university campus, but not the typical one. It was constructed like Oxford University in Great Britain, located in the heavily wooded, rolling Cumberland Mountains of Southern Tennessee. All the buildings were large granite, hand-placed, layer by layer. The campus included a full-sized cathedral.

Beth packed everything imaginable for him. There were pre-addressed postcards, his own phone, and extra money for emergencies. But no news was good news, and the postcards came back in the same suitcase they went in.

There was a definite change in Jason when the family went to spend the fifth week in Sewanee to hear the efforts of the summer camp. There was concert after concert. The most striking was the brass-only concert, held at the stroke of midnight, in the cathedral. The brass split into three groups, each playing in different parts of the cathedral. The sound and reverberations were spine-tingling. The brass was probably heard for miles around. Remember, it was midnight!

Suwanee was a turning point in Jason's life. He repeated it for two more summers. Music became his goal, as well as his passion. Music would drive him to be the best he could for the rest of his life. As he progressed through junior high school, so did his activity in the music program at school. He was a member of the orchestra, the band, and even did a number of paid gigs at the encouragement of the teacher.

He started playing in several orchestras around the state, and even had to become a member of the Musicians' Union to play in one of them. This was a good thing for later on.

He applied to the Tanglewood Summer Music Program and was accepted. What a feather in his cap! Students were accepted from all over the world. The teachers were the "cream-of-the-crop" in the world of music. What a bonding he had with the real world of music. One of his major influences was the large concert at the conclusion of the season. The full orchestra was conducted by a famous, well-renowned conductor.

In his junior year, he had to make a choice of going

to a university with a strong musical program, or going to a music conservatory. He did a lot of research and listened to a lot of suggestions.

He applied to Northwestern, Rice, Julliard, Curtis Institute of Music and many more. He had to take the normal ACTs and SATs, but that was no problem for him. He was accepted at each of these places, but chose Curtis, in Philadelphia. It had as much history as Philadelphia itself.

Curtis paid for everything in school. The only thing Beth and C.J. had to provide was an apartment and food. They found an apartment a few blocks from the college. It had five rooms—each one on top of the other. It had five stories. There was a spiral staircase in the back corner that went up to each room. Two of the rooms, the kitchen and the basement, which housed the washer and dryer, were underground. It was built in the old European brownstone style. Beth wondered, if there were not buildings connected on each side, would this narrow, five-story building be able to exist as a stand-alone. Surely it would topple over.

His trombone teacher was first-chair of one of the leading orchestras in the country. Jason not only excelled at Curtis, but received an advanced degree from Temple University. Music was definitely going to be not only his career, but his life.

Jason became the band music director of one of the largest Catholic music programs in Eastern Pennsylvania;

he joined several professional brass choirs and orchestras. He taught privately. He also continued on in an administrative capacity at Curtis and traveled the world with the orchestra.

By middle age, he had achieved his goal and beyond. Following his college graduation, he married a young lady who was also a student at Curtis. She played the oboe. She had gigs of her own and played with several chamber orchestras. They had two boys, one of which followed in their musical footsteps. The other chose to become a physician, graduating from Colombia, and beyond.

Jason was an administrator, musician, conductor, husband, father, and an individual for motivation of each person whose life he touched.

Beth and C.J. rejoiced in the lives of their children. They only wished they could see them more, but Jason's family chose to move to the suburbs of New Jersey, just across the river from Philadelphia. The physician son moved to the West Coast with his family.

However, they all came to visit Beth and C.J. every chance they had, which was often enough to have a strong family bond. Both of C.J.'s parents had passed away. Friends stayed as important as family.

Chapter 43

Susan was on their high school baseball team, as well as Jessica, which won the state 2-A championship three years in a row, when each of them was on the team. Not only were they super players, but they inspired the whole team to do its best. They were willing to help other players with extra practice.

The families had a scare during Susan's junior year at university. She was "T-boned" by an SUV that ran a stop light while she was going through on the green. She was in the hospital for a month with a broken leg, broken right arm and shoulder. She wasn't able to run and play baseball after that. But, she survived, and that was the important thing.

Susan chose a career in the library sciences and became the director of a large library. She never disrespected Beth's position, though. She knew her love for this profession came from this library in this small hometown and her mom's love for books. Susan became Beth's "go-to" person for advice for keeping up with the latest state-of-the art equipment and computers for the library. This small library had been expanded again by adding a computer room, which housed ten computers for use by the community.

As the years went by, no one questioned Beth's expertise in the library information field. If anyone had been asked, they would have said, yes, sure, she has a degree in Library Science, otherwise, what would she be doing here? No one worried about the fact that she had started working at the library just after her eighteenth birthday and stayed there until her retirement.

Miss Beth just seemed to be a part of the building itself.

C.J. remained the coach of all three teams for thirty years, coaching not only his own two children, but their five children, his grandchildren, as well. Miss Beth remained the assistant, then Director of the library, when Miss Betty retired.

In her junior year at university, Susan and Mark announced their intention to marry. None of the parents, siblings, or friends had any idea they were even dating. When Beth and C.J. burst out laughing, they wondered what was going on. Brian and Kelly just had to join in, catching the joke immediately. Beth explained about C.J.

and her, and then Brian explained about him and Kelly, how they all had secretly dated for at least six months before anyone knew, then there was a sudden wedding announcement.

They were all thrilled, of course. In the years to come, when Jessica and Jason decided to marry, there was added joy.

Jessica had been taught to always be herself, and that decision was up to her. Jason was a good choice for her. Brian and Kelly were overjoyed. It would help keep the connection with all the families going.

Only occasionally through the years did Beth go with C.J., Susan, and Jason to C.J.'s parents' home. They lived in the hometown and Beth was just not willing to go there.

The first time she went, she had to be convinced by C.J. that his parents would not recognize her. She had that short, dark brown hair and those glasses. All she had to do was refrain from laughing that distinctive laugh of hers or give that beautiful smile face on. They might recognize those two things.

But they never did. The excuse for her not coming most of the time was that she had to work, either her regular schedule, or there was something special going on at work she had to attend to—whether there was or not. Fortunately, these visits were only every four months or so.

They got by with it. C.J.'s parents never recognized her. The children knew that their dad's real name was Clayton, so that was no surprise when he was called that. Beth was Beth.

These grandparents passed away, never suspecting that Beth was Misee Sue. Just like the rest of the townspeople, they assumed she had met her death somewhere as the result of foul play, since she never returned to Cedarville.

Chapter 44

Kia was eighty-four years old when she died quietly in her sleep one night. Steven had passed away a couple of years before that. Kia simply went to bed and never woke up, which was the way she always said she wanted to go.

Grandma Susan had passed many years before. She was fifty-eight years old when Beth left home and passed when Beth was forty-one. Grandma was eighty-one. Beth regretted not being able to go to the funeral, but it was in their hometown, so she would not attend. She did allow Kia to tell her about it, how beautiful she had looked in the casket, how peaceful. Beth cried with Kia, for she had loved her Grandma Susan and knew how much Grandma had loved her, never doubting that she caught that ball.

Now, Kia was gone, and so young, everyone thought. Eighty-four was young these days. But, there was a time for everyone.

A time to be born and a time to die.

A time to love, and she had truly been loved.

The whole town, it seemed, turned out for her funeral. The church was packed. Kia was loved by all. She had learned at age fifteen that it was better to listen than to talk. She became an excellent listener. People would come to her to talk about their troubles, with husbands, with children, the in-laws, whatever. She never gave advice, but they all went away thinking how much she had helped them. They never realized they just need someone to talk to, and Kia was that someone. She never repeated anything, and everyone soon realized that.

The church was full and overflowing that morning of the funeral. Music was playing low, as it always does at funerals, and a visual was scrolling slowly on a screen, with photos of Kia's life, mostly with Grandma, Steven, and the kids. No one realized there was not one of her parents or Misee Sue. After all, this was a memorial to Kia.

It was a few minutes past time for the service to begin and everyone was very quiet. The preacher still did not rise to begin the service.

The front doors opened quietly. Someone else was coming in, a few minutes late. Maybe now the service would begin.

An older couple came slowly down the aisle, the gentleman walking with a cane and a small, frail woman on his other arm. His wife, they supposed. They were both very well dressed. She wore all black, including a black hat with a veil that covered her face.

As the couple approached the casket, one of the employees put a stool in front of the casket for the woman to step up on to be able to see into the casket.

The older man reached up and put the veil up on the woman's hat. He helped the woman up on the stool and stepped back. The woman bent over and kissed Kia on the cheek. Then she put both gloved hands on the side of the casket and bowed her head. She remained there for several minutes.

In the meantime, the older gentleman had turned toward her, moving slightly closer, to protect her from falling.

Suddenly, there was an audible gasp in the congregation.

In a whisper that carried clearly across the room, someone said, "That's Clayton Wilkeson! I know it is. I recognize him. He's older, of course, but I know that's him."

The speaker was an older man, yes, Clay's age, who had gone to school with him and played on the baseball team that fateful day.

Just like in the diner that day so long ago, you could have heard a pin drop.

Then, another whisper.

"That must be Misee Sue, I'm sure of it."

Whispers all over the room began.

"It *is* Misee Sue!"

"I thought she was dead long ago, she never came home."

"That doesn't mean she was dead," another said.

"Misee Sue!"

After several minutes more, Beth raised her head, wiped her face, and stepped off the stool, with the help of Clayton and an attendant on the other side. Clay put her veil back in place over her face.

They both turned around, their heads held high. She took Clay's arm as they started down the aisle to the door. They looked straight ahead, never to the right or left.

There was silence as everyone watched them leave. There was no question of following them. After all, this was a funeral, and they were there to honor Kia and her family.

But many people wanted to follow them, just to see where they went, where they lived.

Another funeral home attendant shut the front door when they left and stepped in front of it, barring anyone from leaving, it seemed. That seemed final. Later, many speculated that the funeral home must have known they were coming, since the stool was put there for Misee Sue, so short and petite, to be able to reach Kia in the casket.

Clayton and Misee Sue! After all these years! Who knew?

℘℘℘

Latimer Jones was fifty-nine years old the summer Misee Sue left town. He was spry, still able to do all the work he needed to do around his farm.

Eight years later, he was still baling and putting up hay with the help of one of his sons and two grandsons. He always insisted on going up into the hayloft of the barn, to guide the pulley with each bale on the hook into the hayloft. He just enjoyed doing it.

That summer, for some reason, the bale twisted on the end of the rope. Latimer reached out to grab the bale, which was in motion. He missed the bale, lost his balance, and fell out of the hayloft, tumbling forty feet to the ground.

His son, on the ground, witnessed the fall and tried to be in place by the time his dad reached the ground, to catch him and lessen the fall, but he had to go around several bales, and that took too much time. Latimer hit the ground hard.

He broke his collar bone, an arm, and a leg, each on a different side. He was lucky, his head having missed a farm implement by a few inches. He probably would have been killed on impact with the heavy metal.

However, after going to the hospital and convalescing in a nursing home, he developed complications from the broken collar bone, which was not healing properly. He passed away from an infection that went undetected until too late.

As people did when they knew they were dying, thoughts of his life went through his head. One of his greatest thoughts was about Misee Sue, and how he was responsible for clearing her name and the team being declared the winner of the championship game, after all. He wished she had returned to town, but after he heard how she was treated, he had never blamed her. He was heard calling out her name on occasion with his fever.

Latimer, Susan, and Kia had talked every once in a while through the years.

They took the secret of who cut down The Wilson Bush to their graves.

A promise was a promise.

Chapter 45

C.J. and Beth's driver, Remington, was waiting outside the door as they exited the funeral home. He took Beth's arm and helped her down the steps and helped then each of them into the back seat of the vehicle, Beth first.

They were only a few miles out of town after the funeral when Beth directed Remington to slow down, and then make a left turn at the next road. This was a paved county road. She told him to drive slowly and turn into a cemetery which was coming into view.

He did so. There was a drive down the middle of the cemetery. About halfway down, lanes turned to the right and left, taking a vehicle to outer lanes on each side of this small, country cemetery.

Remington stopped just before they reached these cross lanes, careful not to block the lanes.

He hurried around to help Miss Beth out her side of the vehicle, took her arm as they walked around to Mr. C.J.'s side. He helped him out.

Beth and C.J. locked arms and began looking at the gravestones. Beth had brought up the subject when they knew they were coming to Kia's funeral. Her best bet was that her parents, at least one of them, was buried here. She just didn't know where and did not want to ask anyone.

After criss-crossing several rows, she stopped at a modest gravestone. C.J. let go of her arm and took a few steps backward, allowing her to view this gravesite.

Remington remained about six feet behind C.J. At their ages, he was constantly watching and caring for them. Sometimes they knew it because it was obvious, sometimes they just allowed him to hang around.

This was the first time, in all her lifetime, since she was eighteen years old, that Beth allowed herself to even think about her parents. She had assumed that somewhere along the years, they each had passed away, sooner or later, but Kia never mentioned it and Beth never asked. Kia had always honored Beth's request to never speak of them or their hometown or anyone in it. Except for Grandma, of course, and there was Clay, but that was a different story.

As she gazed at the headstone, with her mother's name, date of birth and date of death, the epitaph caught her attention. It said *Dead of a Broken Heart.*

Whose broken heart? Beth thought. *Mine? Hers? Someone else's?*

For this one time only, from somewhere deep within her, buried and forgotten for…how many years now…sixty-nine years. That long? She guessed so. Beth thought back to that fateful baseball game and the catch of her lifetime. She could feel herself running, running after the ball, having it drop suddenly against her chest, bounce down her forearms, and then miraculously, miraculously, fall into her glove as she gave her hand a twist to the right.

There it was! She'd caught it! She could feel the rush of emotions she felt when she realized she had caught it then felt herself falling as her legs became tangled from the twist as she caught the ball.

Her heart was pounding. This remembering was causing so much anxiety.

But, oh, the thrill of having caught the ball! She relived again the second she realized what her catch meant—their team had won the game and were therefore, State I-A Champions. The capital letters were in her mind because she knew this game was just that important. This town and small school had never won a state championship—ever! Maybe through the years, they had made it to the semi-finals, only to be defeated, so this game was The Game.

She had started shouting, "I caught it, I caught it," even as she fell. She did not remember falling, or the pain of landing on her back, which must have hurt. All she could remember was the joy, the utter excitement, of catching the ball.

She held it up in the air as she continued to shout.

Just then Clayton had come around The Wilson Bush. That stupid, stupid bush, she thought now. But, in a way, that bush helped change and shape her life as she knew it, from age eighteen, that is, and her life had been a good one. She looked his way and saw that he saw her on the ground, holding up the ball, and then she scrambled to her feet. She started jumping around. She remembered the joy of that. What a feeling that had been!

She reached out to him, to have him join in her dance of joy, of triumph, but he took a step back. She stopped dancing. She just stared at him, puzzled.

By that time, others, including the umpire, had come around the bush. The rest of the teams crowded around.

She remembered that umpire shouting, "Did anyone see her catch the ball? Anyone?"

Beth looked around, but no one was nodding. In fact, they were all very still. Then, Marie, the bane of Misee Sue's existence, the hanger-on who had tried to imitate and copycat her since eighth grade, opened her big mouth and said she heard Misee Sue say the other day at school that she would do anything, *anything*, to win this game.

It took her several moments to realize that by *anything* they thought she meant she would lie about this catch, that she had not caught the ball. After all, no one saw her catch it. Maybe she just had picked it up off the ground, fell down, and pretended to catch it.

When a player from the Dover team shouted, "We won, we won," Misee Sue could not believe it. When they started turning and walking away, led by Clayton first, she knew what it meant.

And the look in Clayton's eyes! She shuddered as she remembered that. She remembered the pain, the humiliation, that this action of his cost her. How she was able to forgive him seven years later, she still did not know.

The rest of that evening, the light being turned out on her, the numbness, the walk home unaware, was a blur. Her life for the next week was a blur.

As she stood in front of her mother's grave and remembered those fateful moments, she shook her head. She did not want to remember the rest.

Her mother! Her own loving, wonderful mother, who had rejected her that day!

Beth gave a sob and hung her head.

C.J. had walked up behind her, touched her shoulder. She turned and put her face into his shoulder and cried. She cried about this for the first time in her life, heavy, heart-rendering sobs while C.J. held her and let her cry it out. Maybe this was what she needed after all these years.

Yes, she had forgiven him, but he knew she had not forgotten any of this, not really, not deep down. How could anyone? But whether she cried for her mother, her hometown, or the whole situation, he might never know. If she never spoke of this, he would not ask, just as he had not asked any questions since they were twenty-five years old.

Remington had stayed where he was while she meditated then as she sobbed and turned to C.J. He hurt as she cried, for whatever reason it was. He moved slightly to the right and read the name on the gravestone, but it had no meaning for him. The dates, birth and death, he saw on this right side of the headstone, would be just about right for a parent, though. And she had just attended her sister's funeral. Chances were, this was her mother.

But he would never ask any questions of this beautiful lady.

Chapter 46

As he was waiting for them at the cemetery, Remington remembered the first day they had met. He had been their driver for almost twenty years now. Still, he remembered that first day and all days since as if it and they were yesterday.

He was really down-and-out, and he thought of himself that way. He had heard that term but not really thought of its meaning. Now he knew. It was also said that when a person hit rock bottom, the only way left was up. But Remington did not see a way up. How could you get up when you had nothing to get up with? No money, no decent clothes, nothing. His grandparents were dead, and he had no cousins that he could go to. Everyone needed a big family, if for no other reason than times like this. If he'd had family, someone would take him in. But he had no one.

He finally had to leave home, escape from an abusive stepfather. Where he was going and what would become of him, he didn't know at the time, only that he had to get away. He thought anything would be better than the abuse he received. He was nineteen years old, and his mom had died only a year before. He missed her so much. She had been the "buffer" between him and his mean stepdad.

Remington did look for work, every day, but the man accused him of being lazy, anyway, and asked when was Remington going to get out on his own, get a place of his own. The problem was, this *was* his home. This house was actually in his mother's name, so it belonged to him as much as it did to this man she had married just two years ago, so Remington had determined to stay there.

The stepdad didn't see it that way, though. That last evening he had hit Remington, hard enough that Remington had fallen to the kitchen floor, and that was saying something. Remington was not a small man, and he worked out at the local gym. He knew he needed protection against this man, if it ever came to it. Tonight the man told him to get out of his sight, go to his room, and stay there. And, although Remington was as old as he was, he did as he was told. It was certainly better than being in this man's presence.

After a few minutes, Remington needed to go down

the hall. He did so quietly, pausing at the living room door when he heard his name.

His stepdad was talking on the phone to another man, and Remington was shocked when he heard his stepdad tell the other man to come over in about an hour, so he could see Remington, get acquainted, and if he liked what he saw, he could come on a regular basis. And to bring the money.

Remington, though shocked, knew immediately what that meant. He was to become another man's sex slave. He slipped hurriedly back to his room, just in time. His stepdad came and, ever so quietly, checked to see if Remington was still in his room. Remington made some noise to show him he was so he would go away. He did. Remington heard the TV go on. That meant he had an hour to get away.

Several months back the stepdad had come into his room and said he was going to paint the window sills, it was about time to spruce up the old house. Remington thought that was odd, they didn't look like they needed painting to him, but it happened, of course. A few days later, the windows were stuck, having been painted shut. Remington spent the next month with a chisel and hammer, chipping the paint away so the window would open again, and he greased it so it did not make a sound. He had the thought he might need to get out in a hurry someday. His stepdad would think Remmington could not get out of the house without him seeing him, through the front door—he probably had the back door locked—but Remington would fool him.

He rapidly filled his gym bag with changes of underwear, a couple of T-shirts, an extra pair of jeans, shoes, his toiletries, and snuck out the window.

The state highway was only about a quarter mile from the house. He made it in record time. As soon as he saw a car coming, he held up his thumb. He had heard all the horror stories about hitchhiking, but the alternative was worse. Whatever happened to him now, maybe it would be short-lived, and not the nightmare he could envision. He was sure he would have been locked in his room, ready at any time for the pleasure of the other man, which would probably become men, with his stepdad getting the money for it.

Chapter 47

The first car that approached had slowed down and stopped.

The driver rolled down the window. "Where are you heading, young man?" he asked.

"Anywhere. I don't know," Remington said.

"Well, hop in. Anywhere, it is," the driver said. "I'm Bob Hawkins."

"Remmington."

Hawkins assumed something terrible had happened at home for this young man to be hitching in the dark and didn't mind giving him a ride. Of course, just as Remington had heard from his end the horrors of being picked up by a stranger, so Hawkins knew the dangers of picking up a stranger. But something had compelled him to stop.

The young man looked clean-cut, with clean clothes

and all. But he only had a gym bag. Yeah, he had left in a hurry, all right, only bringing a few extra things with him.

There was silence in the vehicle for several miles. Hawkins looked over and saw a big yawn from Remington.

"There's a pillow and blanket in the backseat. Just reach back between the seats, and you will be able to get them. Why don't you sleep for a while? I'm fresh. I slept during the day because I knew I was going to be driving through the night."

Remington decided that if this man was going to harm him, he probably would have already. He reached back and brought the items to the front.

"You sure?" he asked Mr. Hawkins.

"Positive, you just get a good rest. Do you have a valid driver's license?" he said to Remington.

"Yes, sir, I do. I've never had a ticket or anything," Remington replied.

"Good. I might have you drive when I get tired, so you need to get some sleep. You can't see anything at night, anyway, so you won't miss anything."

Remington didn't care if he missed anything, or not, he just wanted to get far away. Wherever this man let him out, would be okay.

They went up and through the Rockies, through the Eisenhower Tunnel on Interstate 70. Remington didn't wake up and Mr. Hawkins had not awakened him until they were east of Denver.

Hawkins glanced over at him as Remington sat up, removing the blanket.

"You're awake just in time," Hawkins said. "We are coming into Limon. I need gas, and I suppose we both need something to eat. You can wash your face in the bathroom."

They stopped at a convenience stop that had gas and a restaurant, other complete facilities for the use by truckers and other travelers. Hawkins asked him if he wanted to take a shower, but Remington declined. He was okay for a while.

They had a good meal, which Hawkins paid for and Remington protested. He had money for right now. Secretly, he was glad Hawkins had insisted. He didn't know how long his money would last.

Back on the road, Remington drove east from Limon on Interstate 70. They discussed how far Remington would go with Hawkins. Hawkins asked if Remington knew anything about Hays, Kansas. No, he didn't. He had never been there, never had a reason to have been there.

Hawkins was going through there. He suggested if Remington liked the looks and feel of the town maybe that would be a good place to start a new life. Not that he wouldn't take Remington farther, but he wasn't going too much farther himself, to a much smaller town, to visit relatives.

They settled on Hays. After a meal, Hawkins left

Remington at a café. It would be up to Remington from there. Hawkins insisted on giving Remington some money when they parted, forcing it into his hand.

When Remington looked later, he was surprised to see two one-hundred dollar bills. He tucked them away in the small front pocket of his blue jeans. He promised himself not to use them unless he absolutely had to.

He had to.

He had been in Hays for three months, and it had been all he could do to beg a job a day at a time for a meal, and maybe a storage shed to sleep in. One day he would wash dishes for a meal, the next mop a floor. He didn't seem to be able to find part-time, much less full-time anywhere, not even dishwashing. For three days now, even the occasional dishwashing and mopping job had not materialized.

He was hungry. He had not had a shower in a week. He knew what he smelled like. His second change of clothing was just as dirty as these he was wearing. He had been more than grateful to Bob Hawkins for taking him much farther away from his stepdad than he had dreamed. They both thought that he would be able to find some job in Hays. But, like many towns and cities in the country, there was high unemployment. Even for the most menial jobs, there were more applicants than jobs available.

He wasn't a bad young man. He wasn't a druggie and didn't want to be. But he was at the point that he knew he might have to start dealing or sell his body on the street if something didn't turn up. And the thought of that second option was the worst thing he could think of. Maybe not for everyone, he realized, but for him. After all, that was what he had run away from.

He sat on the curb with his head hanging down, just staring at the pavement. He figured the only reason a police officer hadn't stopped and told him to move on, was the fact that he wasn't panhandling. He wasn't holding up a sign and didn't have a cup in front of him for people to put money in, or anything like that. They probably thought he was just sitting and waiting to be picked up by a friend or someone.

Then a pair of women's shoes stopped in front of him. Attached to the feet were nice, black slacks.

He remembered thinking, *Old lady slacks, old lady shoes.*

Chapter 48

Expecting the feet to point toward the street, in anticipation of crossing it, he was surprised when they moved and pointed at him. At the same time, a voice said, "Young man, are you hungry?"

The voice was so beautiful, so musical with a soft lilt, that he looked up immediately. He guessed right about the old lady part, but what a beautiful old lady!

"If you're hungry, I know of several places we could go to eat. Your choice, of course."

"Yes, I'm hungry," was the simple reply.

"How long has it been since you have eaten?"

"Three days. I think," he said.

"Then come on, let's go."

He found himself getting up, and it took an effort. He was very weak, but he noted the fact that she gave him the courtesy of letting him get up by himself, instead of trying to help him, letting him keep his dignity. After all, an old lady helping a young man! What a shame that would be.

She looked up one side of the street and down the other. "I see lots of fast food places and other smaller restaurants. What type of food would you like? There's an Italian place, and a Mexican—"

"Mexican," he replied. "Oh, sorry, I didn't mean to interrupt you, it's just that—"

"I know, I know, it's your favorite." She laughed, and, to him, it was the most beautiful laugh he had ever heard, just like it always was and had been to another young and now older man. "Why go any further naming places, right? Mexican, it shall be. Let's go."

He marveled at the fact that she walked right beside him down the street, chatting away. He knew what he smelled like, yet here she was, almost shoulder to shoulder. The waiter looked at them funny when they entered the restaurant, but he recognized a lady when he saw one, so this must be an okay situation.

She suggested he order something light, although she assured him he could have anything he wanted.

"I only think it's a good idea to eat something light, since you haven't eaten in three days. Your stomach will not be ready for something heavy or a lot of anything."

He ordered just one taco, and she approved of the choice.

"You'll have much more to eat after this, but you have to get your stomach ready for it, first," she said, mysteriously.

He wondered what she meant, but the taco had arrived.

She was right. He could only eat half of it and a few drinks of the soda he had ordered.

He apologized for wasting her money.

"Don't worry about it," she said.

Then she asked him to tell her his story. He found himself telling her everything, about the death of his mother, even his opinion that it was caused by the stepdad and his abuse. She nodded periodically as he talked. The talk exhausted him.

She made no comment or judgment.

"Do you have a valid driver's license?" she asked, to his surprise.

"Why, yes, I do have that," he said.

"May I see it?"

"Sure," he said, as he dug in his front pocket.

It had not taken him very long on the street to know that you did not carry anything in a back pocket. It wouldn't be there when you reached for it the next time.

She saw that he had given her his correct name. The license was good, from Utah, and had an expiration date a year from then.

She nodded. "My husband and I were just talking the other day about how we need to hire a driver. We're both getting to the point that driving, especially in any type of heavy traffic at all, scares us. We hesitate too much." She laughed. Old people drivers, that's what they had become. "Would you like to become our driver? Full-time, permanent? We would furnish you with room and board—a garage apartment it is, behind our house. You would have regular hours, but drive on special occasions when we asked you to. You could not be loud or have loud parties, no lady friends staying over, or anything like that in the apartment. We would buy you a computer and TV for your entertainment, but expect you not to watch porn or adult movies, or anything like that. We just don't think that's necessary. Could you live with that?" She named a salary, on top of the benefits. Then she laughed. "Oh, I forgot. We live in a small town in northwestern Kansas. I guess I should have asked if you could live with that!"

The garage apartment was the same she had moved into when she was just eighteen. When Miss Clarissa passed away, her children did not want to live in that small town, so they put her house up for sale. Before the sale went public, the real estate agent called Beth. She heard Beth say several times that if she had the chance, she wanted to buy Miss Clarissa's place.

Beth and C.J. had lived there for twenty-five years now. Their children had always stayed in the apartment when they visited, but now they would just have to stay in the big house and whoever had to could rent a room.

She let Remington drive home. She said he might as well get used to this vehicle, he would be driving it. He had never driven a nice luxury Lincoln like this, but he loved it.

She didn't say much as they made the trip home.

Chapter 49

As they went through the back door, she called out, "C.J., dear, we have company."

C.J. never knew what to expect with Beth. She introduced Clay to Remington as C.J., so he knew that was what he would call him.

Mr. C.J. Miss Beth.

When C.J. saw a dirty young man, he didn't bat an eye but extended his hand in greeting. Remington loved this man as quickly as he had Beth.

"This is our new driver. Remember, we said we needed one. He'll live in the apartment. But, first," she said, as she turned to Remington. "how about a shower, shave, and shampoo? The three S's." She laughed again. Remington would grow to love that laugh. "I know C.J.'s clothes will fit you. He'll rustle up something while you shower. And I'm starved."

She turned toward the kitchen. Clay would take charge from here.

The next day, they went shopping for clothes. Remington asked if he could have several of the same type of shirt, so he could wear that every time he was driving them somewhere. It would identify him with Mr. C.J. and Miss Beth.

He didn't know it when he asked that, but he soon learned that being identified with this couple automatically earned him the respect and friendship of the town. They simply accepted him. He had never experienced that before but welcomed the feeling. It was just another reason to love this couple.

When he had been with them four years, he walked around the house to where they were sitting on the front porch. He went into the kitchen and returned with tea. They never minded him doing that. He was family.

"May I ask you something?" he asked.

They turned toward him. "Of course, Remington, dear, what is it?" Beth asked.

"Well, I've met someone, someone special, and I would like your approval."

Beth sat up, leaning toward him with a smile. "Why, dear, you don't need our approval for your relationships, beyond the rules of the house, of course."

"Yes, I think I do," Remington argued. "The special

someone is Alicia Conrad. She's a waitress at the diner. She's from here, she said, left home, and she's gone through a rough patch in her life, I know, but she told me she has changed and wanted to come back to her hometown. I take it from what she told me that it has not always been a bed of roses for her, either here or in the city. So, I need you to approve of her. Or not, whatever the case may be. If you don't, I won't continue the rela-tionship, of course. We've…well…talked several times. I don't know if you could call them dates, or not."

He looked at them expectedly.

Beth knew he wanted and needed their approval of this young lady. Well, not so young. She would be…what?…twenty-seven, twenty-eight, maybe? Beth did some quick math. They were friends with her grand-parents and heard what the parents had said about Alicia. It was the usual story of a young lady wanting to leave a small town for "more," then having to return after finding nothing "out there" for herself.

Beth liked her, actually. She seemed like a nice enough young lady. "We know the family, and we know her, of course," she answered. "She always waits on us at the diner, as you know. I—we—" She looked at C.J., who nodded his agreement. "—don't see anything wrong in your dating her. I sense there could be more than just a desire to date her, though," she said, looking at Reming-ton with a smile on her face.

"Okay, I admit to already having serious feelings for

her. Which is another point. Can a person be so sure of someone after so short a time?" he asked.

"Oh, yes, of course," Beth said. "Love has no time frame, and no rhyme or reason, for that matter."

She looked at C.J., and the look that passed between them let Remington know there was a lot to their story. But he would never ask. Maybe someday he would hear their story.

He dated Alicia and, after six months, asked C.J. and Beth again for their approval for him to marry Alicia, which he knew he didn't need, not really, but for some reason, it seemed appropriate to ask them.

C.J. and Beth were elated, of course. Remington and Alicia would live in the garage apartment. C.J. and Beth insisted on that. Remington hoped for that but had been ready to move out, if it came to that. He inwardly breathed a sigh of relief when they insisted he and Alicia live there. C.J. and Beth would continue to pay the utilities and expenses as part of Remington's salary until such time as they would like to have the apartment and a small area of land around it deeded over to them. It would be C.J. and Beth's wedding present to them. At that point, they would take responsibility for everything—insurance, taxes, and maintenance. C.J. still helped with the expense of maintenance through the years, but did it gladly.

It took them two years to decide they could afford the care of the property, and the deed—no pun intended, said C.J.—was done. At the same time, Remington and

Alicia announced they were expecting a child, so there was another reason to celebrate. Alicia continued to work on the wait staff at the diner, and the owner let her work on weekends after the baby, a boy, was born.

C.J. and Beth gave Remington a substantial raise in salary when he married and at regular intervals thereafter. He and Alicia were very content to live in the apartment, to her credit. She had "learned her lesson," so to speak, from her adventurous years in the big city. She knew now what she had in her hometown and lived life everyday counting her blessings, especially her love for Remington. She had grown to love C.J. and Beth as much as he did. It was like they had rescued them both.

Now that they had started a family, they expanded the apartment, converting the garage into a living room/family room. The former living room became a dining room. They had enough space behind to make two bedrooms with a connecting bathroom between them across the width of the apartment and twenty feet deep. It left only about twelve feet before the next property line, but no one went behind there, anyway, so it only had to be mowed and trimmed, and there was room to do that.

Remington and Alicia wanted two children, at least. They ended up with three, which was just right for the space they had provided, plus a guest room.

He didn't know it at the time, but C.J. and Beth left the "big house" to them in their will. This was with the approval of the children, of course. They each had their own large homes, one in this small town and the other not too far away. They would always have enough space and be able to provide for their own families. They knew how much Remington and Alicia and their children meant to their parents. The children had accepted them as family, also.

A family and friends gathering was always a large, wonderful event. Through the years, they never thought of or called them reunions. How could they be reunions when they saw each other all the time?

Remington had hung back the first time they went to Brian and Kelly's just to "sit on the porch and relax," but they wouldn't allow it. From the first time he drove C.J. and Beth there, he had a special chair that became his "spot." Through these friends, he learned to enjoy the beautiful Kansas sunsets. He learned how to relax, laugh, and love. He agreed that the sweet tea Brian learned to make from his mother was the best of all.

Brian and Kelly welcomed the children through the years. The back porch became wall-to-wall chairs, rockers, and swings, but what was it for, anyway? And toys. Don't forget the toys.

Remington had also taken over the lawn care for C.J. and Beth. He did it gladly, but they insisted on paying him the same, if not more, than the lawn service had charged. The lawn service had grown to have so many accounts, C.J. and Beth had been willing to give them up. There was always a neighborhood teenager around who wanted to make extra money. When Remington wanted to do it, it was a "win-win" for all of them.

He suddenly realized, as he watched his couple with care this day at the cemetery, that, in the over twenty years he had worked for them, he had never heard the reason Miss Beth had been in Hays that day. She had never said.

But he knew then and now, if he had ever asked, she would have just laughed that wonderful laugh of hers and would have probably said something like "Well, I was there for you, of course. Don't you know that?"

He would have laughed, also, and agreed with her. It would have been the truth, if maybe not all of it. She *had* been there for him and rescued him. He would never forget those shoes that came into view as his head hung down. Old lady shoes, he had thought at the time, but with the most wonderful old lady in the world attached to them! He had not seen her wear those shoes for many years now, but he bet she still had them.

That day he had been rescued, as he always thought of it. He had been nineteen years old. He figured he wouldn't have ten more years with them, simply because of their ages, but who knew that sort of thing? They were both eighty-seven. But he would do anything for this couple, especially Beth. She had rescued him. He would take care of both of them until the end.

Then he could face anything. Beth had taught him that.

He helped them back into the car.
They would never travel this way again.

Chapter 50

Two weeks later, C.J., Beth, and Kelly were at Kia's house. Remington had driven them, of course. Kia's husband had passed about eight years before. Since Kia's death had happened suddenly, her children would not be able to come to the house for a couple of more weeks to dispose of her things. One of Kelly's farm hands had driven her here in the pickup to help move furniture, should she choose some heavy items from the house.

Kia's children told Beth to take whatever she and the others wanted. Kia had told them about certain items that would go to Beth, should she, Kia, go first. They really didn't care what Beth took. One of Kia's children was leaning toward moving into the house, but it was too early to make a decision. That would come after the grieving process was over.

C.J. went to Kia's study, the room that had also been the office for Steven. Kelly went to the garage, to see if some of the tools, or whatever, could be used on the farm.

Brian had passed away some years back, but Kelly still had several farm hands that kept the farm profitable.

Remington and Kelly's man sat down on stools at the kitchen counter. They would just stay out of the way while everyone was busy, until and if they were needed. Then they decided to fill the tanks of their respective vehicles. Kelly's man left first, and then Remington would go. That way, there would always be one of them, if either three of the older friends needed help.

Beth went to Kia's bedroom. She paused in the doorway, sensing her sister's presence in this room. She also felt Steven, who had shared this room with Kia for their adult lives, with never a thought of one of them sleeping elsewhere, like the sofa after a spat. If they had been fussing at each other during the day, though never a real "fight," they always made up before they went to bed—as, Kia said, the Bible told them to. It was a good plan which had served them well through the years.

This room looked like Kia and was different from the last time Beth had seen it, but that was many years ago, Beth realized. The walls were painted a subtle gold, probably with a name only the paint companies could come up with. Did these corporations pay someone full-time to come up with all the names you saw on the walls of the hardware stores?

What a thought to have!

The curtains matched the comforter and pillow shams on the king-sized bed. This bedroom suite was new. Beth recognized the style as being Amish-made. She knew the quality and price of this. One of the kids would surely want this. She would tell them that, if no one did, she would take it. But, it was so nice, she felt the children should have "dibs" on it before she did.

The pattern on the curtains and bed items was a small, light blue-and-gold flower, typical of Kia. She did not like large, loud prints.

Beth had no idea where to start looking, so she decided to start with the dresser. She ran her hand down the length of the top. In two weeks' time, only a sprinkling of dust was on the surface. Again, this was typical of Kia. It was as if Kia had completely cleaned the house the day before she passed away.

Maybe she did, Beth thought. *She wouldn't have wanted to die leaving the house messed up.*

Beth smiled at the thought. Kia had always been such a neat person, even as a little girl. She had never been accused of being lazy or a bad housekeeper. Beth was neat, but was a little more lax than Kia.

For no particular reason, Beth pulled out the bottom drawer on the right. The only thing in the drawer was what looked like a jewelry box. Beth thought that was an awkward place to put jewelry, but maybe it contained items that Kia had quit wearing in her older years. Favorite pieces came and went, Beth had to admit that. But Kia would have to stoop and bend then straighten up to get any jewelry out of here.

That particular motion did not come any easier as a person grew "less young."

Beth opened it. It had certainly been a jewelry box at one time, compete with liner on the bottom to keep anything from scratching. On one side, there were little raised grooves for rings, but no rings were there. Instead of jewelry, there were just a few items, mementos of Kia's past. Beth recognized a bracelet she had given Kia when they were children. There was a small pocket knife that Grandma had given her. Grandma, ever the practical one, had said you never knew when a knife might come in handy. She always carried one herself.

Beth was about to put the few items back in the box and close the lid when she spied a piece of paper sticking up in one corner. It was just the tiniest piece, but certainly indicated a larger piece of paper underneath the lining.

Now, what could Kia have been keeping secretly hidden under there? Beth wondered.

It was a page from an old newspaper. Probably an article Kia particularly liked. Beth gingerly opened the paper.

An article on the bottom left-hand corner caught her attention. The caption read:

1-A State Baseball Championship Game
Overturned in Cedarville, KS.

In an unprecedented decision, the Kansas State Baseball Commissioner for high schools overturned a recent win by Dover for the state 1-A championship.

Coach Smith, of the Cedarville team, presented the commissioner with eye-witness information that refuted the winning decision the evening of the championship game, which was held in Cedarville. The eye-witness, Latimer Jones, signed a sworn affidavit that what he witnessed was the truth and real story of a "miracle" catch by a young lady, the center fielder on the home team.

It seems there is a large, extremely bushy shrub in the middle of center field on the baseball field, about ten feet from the back center field line. Every competing team has been willing to sign their agreement to play on this field with the bush in the back middle, in order to play here, and they have done so for the last fifty years. Of course, each year the bush has grown bigger, but the agreement still stands. It seems there are certain rules that apply to the bush, such as "if the ball lands and lodges in the bush, with no way to be reached by a player, this is an automatic double." As inconceivable as it sounds, there are other rules that apply to this bush!

It has never been ideal, but each team decided they had the same advantage, or disadvantage, as the case may be.

During the game in question, the centerfielder, Misee Sue Stone, ran behind the bush in order to catch a fly ball. She started yelling that she had caught it, but by the time another player, the first player around the bush, Clayton Wilkeson, saw her, she was on the ground, holding up the ball in the air and yelling "I caught it, I caught it, we won."

However, when the umpire asked if anyone saw her catch it, no one had witnessed it. It appeared that, with the way the ball was going in the air, it would have dropped behind the bush and there could have been no way she could have caught it like she said. It seems no one believed her.

Everyone turned away, and the umpire declared Dover the winner of the game.

Jones had been gone from early morning the next morning after the game until the next Saturday morning, when he went into the diner in Cedarville, saw Miss Stone's father, and started congratulating him on the "miracle" catch of Misee Sue. That started the ball rolling (excuse the pun) for the decision to overturn the winner. Although Dover was outraged, entering an appeal, Cedarville rejoiced with a parade and victory celebration. However, at the time of this writing, the young lady, Misee Sue Stone, has disappeared.

Beth could not believe what she just read. She was a fast reader and had read it all in a few seconds.

"Oh! Oh, no!" Beth cried.

Her hands went to her mouth. The newspaper fell onto her lap as she sat down on the side of the bed. It was a good thing the bed was so near, or she may have fallen.

Chapter 51

At the first "Oh," three heads went up immediately.

At the second "Oh," all three friends were in motion.

C.J. was the closest, just down the hall in the study, but he had to look around for his cane, take three steps to it, and get it in place, before he could start toward the room where Beth was.

Remington, sitting on the stool in the kitchen, was in motion in a flash, racing down the hall to the bedroom.

In the garage, Kelly heard Beth's cry and started running, but had to go through the mudroom and kitchen.

That put Remington the first one inside the bedroom door, but with C.J. and Kelly on his heels. Remington stepped aside as C.J. appeared behind him.

All three said, "Beth, are you okay? What happened? Are you okay?"

"Tell us, what happened?" C.J. repeated as he went to her side. He sat down beside her on the bed and put his arms around her. "Are you okay? What happened?"

Kelly and Remington sat down on the other side of the bed.

"Look! Look!" Beth said, as she handed the newspaper page to C.J. "Look at the article in the lower left-hand corner. I can't believe it. Did you know about this? You had to know about it. Why didn't you say something?"

C.J. quickly saw what she was talking about.

The overturn decision.

Kia had kept the article.

"Where did you get this?" C.J. asked.

"It was down in the bottom of this box," Beth answered, gesturing toward the box. "Just a tiny bit of paper showed up from under the lining, but I wondered what Kia might have kept under there, so I brought it out. I can't believe it. You've known all these years!"

"Misee Sue, remember what you told Kia and what you also told me all those many years ago now. You never, and I mean *never*, wanted to hear about anything about Cedarville or about anyone there. Kia said she tried to tell you things through the years, but you always cut her off, never wanting to hear it. She said the only thing she could ever discuss with you was your Grandma Susan and things pertaining to her. I know Kia wanted to tell you things, but you never allowed it. Neither would you allow me to say anything. Remember?"

Remington had heard C.J. call Miss Beth "Misee Sue," through the years and wondered about it but just figured it was a pet name or something.

"But look at this date on the paper," Beth said, drawing C.J.'s attention to the top of the page. Kia had kept the whole page which showed the original date. "This is just two weeks after the game, a week after I left."

"Yes, yes, it is. I see that, and I know that. And, yes, I've known all about this, the whole circumstances, ever since that Saturday that Latimer Jones came into the diner, but I could never tell you."

"This also means that if I had been in town just two days later, I would have heard Mr. Jones say he saw me catch that ball. His land does border the ball field, and his barn is right there, right past center field. I didn't know he was there, watching. Of course, I was watching the ball," Beth said. "Why didn't he come forward right then, tell everyone what he saw?"

"Are you ready to hear this? Hear all about it? I remember it as if it happened yesterday. How could I ever forget it? I lost you that day, I know it. I thought I would never get you back, never see you again."

C.J. had handed the article to Kelly, who read it and passed it to Remington.

Remington was getting more and more confused by the second, but he noticed that Kelly was just sitting there calmly, just listening. Did she know what they were talking about? Remington knew they had been friends most of their lives, he just didn't know exactly how long that was, when they had met, or how. He knew he was getting ready to hear something very interesting about this couple he loved dearly.

"I think I need to know, now that I've seen this article," Beth said. She hesitated slightly, but only slightly. "Yes." She nodded. "I'm ready to hear everything, Clay, dear." She looked into C.J.'s eyes. Yes, she was ready. "Start with Latimer coming into the diner. Where had he been all week since the game? Had he really been gone?"

"Yes," C.J. replied. "I was in the diner when he came in and found a stool at the counter. You remember that last stool he used to sit in at the end of the counter?"

Beth nodded. Mr. Jones was a fixture there on Saturday at noon.

"He was late that day and had to sit in the middle of the counter. That's why, I guess, he was able to look up and see us in that mirror. I was having lunch with your parents that day. We were in that booth right in the middle of the front window. You know the one I mean?" he asked.

Again, Beth nodded. The one big enough for a large family. Why were just the four of them there?

"Suddenly, he whirled around on that stool and yelled at your dad. 'John!' he yelled out. Of course, John Jenkins and John Wampler both looked up but went back to eating when they saw Mr. Jones looking at your dad. Mr. Jones started in asking us about that miracle catch you made, wasn't that something, he had seen it with his own eyes, and couldn't believe it, but there it was, bouncing around on your chest, down your arms, and finally, with a flick of your left wrist, you had that ball in your glove, but then you fell flat on your back, but never lost the ball. You held it up in the air the whole time. He was really going on about it, how he hadn't ever made a catch like that, and he played a mean game of ball back in his day. When he finally paused for breath, your dad interrupted, saying, 'What do you mean, you saw it?'

"Mr. Jones explained that he heard the roar of the crowd and stepped out that back door of his barn just in time to see the ball drop and you dance around and catch it. He said he knew we had won the game, but just then his cow mooed from the front of the barn, so he went back in and shut that back door. There is a tack room…or whatever you want to call it…right there, and a door out of that room leading to the main part of the barn, and he closed the second door, also. He said he started talking to Bessie as he walked to the front of the barn, so he couldn't hear the rest of the game at that point.

"He got up very early the next morning because his nephew and wife were picking him up to go up Nebraska to visit for a week with his brother. That's why he didn't know the game had been awarded to Dover or hear that no one believed you. He didn't hear anything about our part of Kansas up there in Nebraska. Why should he have? As soon as he got into town, he came right to the diner to eat. He had even been served by Sally before he saw us, then all hell broke loose! I was the first one to jump up and say 'You know what this means, don't you? We won the game! We need to find Coach. Where is he?' I looked around the diner. Coach and his wife always ate there on Saturdays like everyone else. Why wasn't he there? I remember thinking. Someone said he had gone to the lake that weekend with his wife. I said 'Who's coming with me?' I think every man in that diner climbed into vehicles. We stopped for gas, and off we went to get Coach, to tell him what Mr. Jones had just said."

"You all drove all the way to Lake Cowley? Isn't that where Coach's cabin was?" Beth asked.

"We sure did, and I was so happy, so happy, thinking that now you would forgive us all for ignoring you, for shunning you, for calling you a liar. I was going to tell you how much I loved you and never let you go again. I was going to beg your forgiveness for not believing you. That Marie! Why did she have to say that? Did you know she followed me around for a year and a half at university before I finally told her, in no uncertain terms and in front of several people, that she would never be you, never be Misee Sue, and to leave me alone or I would call the police."

Beth found herself smiling, imagining the look that probably appeared on Marie's face. Where was she, Beth wondered, at age eighty-seven? Still jealous of everyone around her? Still alive? Then Beth grew serious again.

"Anyway," C.J. said, "we all drove to the lake and called Coach to come in off the water. We could see his boat just slightly on the horizon. He was very excited to hear what Mr. Jones witnessed. He immediately called the commissioner, who he knew personally. It seems they were college buddies, or something. Anyway, they made an appointment for that Monday. Within a couple of days, the commissioner made the decision to overturn the ball game and give the win to Cedarville. You can imagine the yelling in Dover!" C.J. laughed at the thought. "But this final decision stood, because of Mr. Jones."

"I wish I could thank Mr. Jones personally for clearing my name, but I know he would no longer be with us."

"No," C.J. said simply. He told her the details of Mr. Jones's death and the year he passed away—many years ago.

She just shook her head.

"If you had just waited two more days before you left, Misee Sue, you would have known the truth, as we all learned it. You could have stayed home," C.J. said.

Chapter 52

Home?" Beth asked, incredulously. "You call that home? That week I went through? If there is a hell on earth, I went through it that week. You will never, and I do mean *never*, know what that week was like, after the game. The shunning and ignoring of me by my own mom and dad. They wouldn't even look at me, much less talk to me. No one answered my texts, not even Amber. And you, not even you. That look you gave me the night of the game, so full of loathing and…and…whatever—" She gave a dismissive gesture in the air with her right hand. "Where were you, when I needed you the most, above everyone else, where were you? And don't you remember graduation? No one responded to my valedictorian speech, not even you. No one made the special sign for our class, not even you.

When I walked out of the auditorium—walked out of the school—my mind was made up. I just had to wait for the right time to make my move. I gave the family, and you, by the way, until Thursday night to talk to me, but no one did. Not even Amber, who I thought would be my best friend for life.

"The only one who talked to me, and I asked her to do it by text, of course, because she had to live with our parents, was Kia. Kia told me right away that she believed me, that if I said I caught the ball, she believed me. She said I was the most honest person she knew. That could have been just the little sister talking, but I don't think so. She was just like that, and all her life, as you know. Her loyalty knew no bounds. Well," Beth continued, "this article is an excellent example of her loyalty. I asked her early on never to talk about our hometown or anyone in it, not even you, Clay, and she didn't. Not ever. I just didn't need it."

She had shared with Clay the time she first called Kia, when Kia went to university.

"She could have told me about you during that last year I was at university when she was a Freshman, but she didn't," C.J. said. "Yes, definitely loyal. Maybe she thought you didn't love me anymore."

"Maybe," Beth responded. "That's a possibility. But she found out the truth of that when we finally got back together. You said it would have been easy, Clay, if I had just stayed two more days and everything would have gone back to normal. But you're wrong. I would not have just automatically fallen back into your arms. I was not able to forgive you, the hurt was so great. The betrayal I felt by your actions and silence was almost unbearable. I really don't think I would have gotten over that if we had been so close in distance, at that time. And my parents. Can you imagine the pain, the rejection I felt? No, everyone was a week too late!"

She smiled at C.J. "I needed those years away from that total situation. I needed the years away from you to realize, when we did meet at that deli, that I could love you again. It just took me even more time. That six months."

"But thank God we found each other again, and you realized in that time, those *years*, that you could forgive and love me," he said. He looked over at Kelly. "I'm so glad you and Brian decided to marry that day and in that place. Beth and I might never have found each other again."

"I don't believe that," Kelly answered. "I believe it was meant to be. But I'm glad to have been a part of it." She turned and looked at Beth. "Brian told me, of course, about the first time you two met, through Gail. If you had not left your hometown when you did, you would not have come to Gail's, met Brian. You would not have signaled me over to join you guys at your table that day at that deli, and we—Brian and I—would not have met, at least probably not. We would have met someone else and maybe married, or had lovers, but life would not have been the perfect life it has been for Brian and me. If we had not seen little Susan and loved her so much, we would not have adopted Jessica, and she would not have grown up to marry Jason, and all our lives would have been totally different. And the lives you have touched and influenced in Evansville know no end. Think of all the children you influenced throughout all these years by being at the library. At that small, wonderful library in Evansville. You opened up so many worlds of possibilities for so many children. I didn't know until right now that you were the Misee Sue of this story. I've always known you as Beth. Did Brian know? You *are* this Misee Sue, aren't you?"

"No, Brian did not know. He was introduced to me as Beth Connors, and that's all he ever knew. And, yes, I am the Misee Sue in this story. But wait. Let me show you."

Beth reached for her purse. She turned it over and let everything fall out of it onto the bed. When everything was out, she rummaged around inside for a minute, then came up with a folded piece of paper.

"Look at this," she said, handing the paper to Kelly.

She unfolded it. She saw the birth certificate of Misee Sue Stone.

Remington would recognize the name of her mother as the name he saw on the gravestone where they stopped last week.

Kelly sent Beth a silent question, which she understood.

"Yes, show Remington. He's been a part of the family for twenty years."

Remington took the paper and looked at it, then handed it back to Kelly.

"I'm remembering something," Kelly said. "It was something one of the grands said after he came back from baseball camp one summer, oh, many years ago, of course, when he was a teenager. He said some of the guys told a story about a girl on a baseball team during a 1-A championship game who made a miracle catch but, because of a large bush growing in the middle of center field, no one believed her, so the other team won, then it was overturned. The name was Misee Sue. You definitely are the Misee Sue of the article. All the dates check out, your birthdate, the date on the newspaper article, which means you were eighteen that year," she said, as she handed the paper back to her.

Remington turned to C.J. "So that means you are the Clayton Wilkeson of the article. C.J. Wilkes. Clay. It all makes sense. And the times through the years you slipped, Mr. C.J., and called Miss Beth 'Misee Sue,' all those times make sense now, too. It was hard at times, I can imagine, to call her Beth when you grew up calling her Misee Sue. And I'm just guessing that the two of you grew up together."

"You guessed right. We did. We loved each other

since third grade and made such wonderful plans to go to university together, to marry and have the most wonderful family in the world. Which we did, of course, have the most wonderful family in the world, I mean—"

"That's not true," Kelly interrupted. "Brian and I had the most wonderful family and now the grandchildren."

They all smiled. At least they were getting back to normal.

Chapter 53

"Miss Beth?" Remington asked gently.

They all turned to look at him.

"I've put all this together by what's been said here, but…" He looked at Beth so hesitantly. "I mean, do you wish, right now, that you had waited those two days, that your life had been different?"

Beth realized instantly what he was asking, what he was saying. "Oh, no, Remington, dear. Never," she said, without hesitation.

Remington did not know what he would have felt if she had hesitated with her answer. It meant that much to him.

"Never through all these years," she continued, "all…well, sixty-nine of them now…and not now, with this new information I just learned about that day and that following week." She bent her head, and a frown appeared between her brows. "I just realized something. I never told you why I was in Hays that day, did I?"

"No, ma'am, you never have, and I would never..." He didn't finish.

Beth finished for him. "And you would never ask, I know, Remington, you are so considerate. But, you must have wondered."

"Yes, Miss Beth, I have."

"Well, here it is. My local doctor found a spot on an X-ray that he couldn't identify. He asked his partner, who also couldn't identify what it was. They referred me to a specialist that came to Hays only one day a week. I had to make an appointment for three months from when I called, and it was a tense three months. C.J. and I imagined all sorts of scenarios, including cancer, of course. People always think of cancer when a spot is detected. My appointment in Hays included the physical exam, more tests, blood work, the whole works. I was asked to wait for three hours, and I would have the results. I was willing to do that, of course, to know what the spot was. I couldn't believe it when they specialist did not find anything wrong with me. He consulted with another specialist that came with him each week. There was no spot on the X-ray or MRI, nothing wrong with my blood work and numbers. They found nothing. They decided it was either a spot on the film, a computer glitch, or I had been miraculously healed during the last three months. They never thought that my family doctor was incompetent, just that everything had changed. But we both know why I was there, don't we, dear?" she asked quietly.

"Yes, Miss Beth, you were there for me. You saved me," he replied.

She swore she saw tears forming in his eyes. "And you saved us. What would we have done without you, and then Alicia, then the children, through the last twenty years? I can't imagine it without you. From the instant I saw you, you were a part of me, of us." She looked at C.J., who nodded his agreement. "I'll admit, though, that I started to walk past you. I saw you when I first started walking down the sidewalk toward you. There was not that much foot traffic in downtown Hays at that time of day. I almost walked past, but something made me stop. My heart jumped in my chest, literally, and I had to stop. My, how dirty and stinky you were."

"I know." Remington grinned. "But you never said a word about it. I loved you for that. Well, for other things, too."

"So, what were *you* doing there? You've never told us all about that—"

Remington laughed. "And you've never asked."

He told them the story about his stepdad and the man who picked him up and drove him to Hays. How he found work from place to place, almost day to day, but could never find anything permanent or full-time. It was a wonder he did not get sick during that time. Only the fact that he started out so healthy with a young man's body saw him through those months. He had not worked for a week or eaten in three days, and he had no money at all. He was ready to go on the streets. A man he had met on the streets told him just that morning there might be a job, he had heard, downtown at the cafeteria in the physicians' building. He came as soon as he heard, but the job had been filled just an hour before. They told him he could fill out an application just in case this guy didn't work out, but he had no phone and no address, so how could he fill out an app?

"I was starting to walk back to the other area of town, when I felt so dizzy, I almost fell down. I grabbed that light post and sat down on the curb, hard. I told myself I would sit for a while, and then I would have the strength to get up and go on. I'm not sure I would have, though. I just barely had the energy to get up when you talked to me. And thank you for not helping, for giving me the courtesy of getting up by myself." The last he said to Beth. "And there you were, old ladies' shoes and all!"

Beth laughed. "I loved those shoes. They were so comfortable. I wore them until they wore out."

"I know I would not have been saved that day if you had waited for two days," Remington responded quietly with a grin.

"I know," she said. "Our lives, every one of us—" She made a gesture to encompass them all. "—have been lived as they have meant to be. All sixty-nine years, two months, and thirteen days of them." She smiled at C.J. "Right?"

"Okay, okay, I'll give you the day."

"You've lost me again," Remington said.

"Me, too," Kelly said.

Beth and C.J. just laughed. They looked at each other, reaching for and holding hands.

"There's one thing," Kelly said.

They turned to her.

"What's that?" Beth asked.

"It's my opinion that you should destroy your original birth certificate, the one showing you as Misee Sue. What are your children and grandchildren going to think if they find that when you die, and they will probably find it. They won't know who you are, and it will mess with their minds, wondering who their parents and grandparents really are, and all that. Just think about it. By the way, since this is a day of telling the truth of the past, how did you come to be Beth and not remain Misee Sue? I think Brian must have known, but he never said. You seem to have had many people who remained loyal to you and all your secrets throughout your lifetime. But, then, I know first-hand how you inspire friendship and loyalty."

"Thank you, Kelly," Beth said. She told her how Gail's mother offered her the birth certificate that she had now, as Elizabeth Ann Conners. She found another paper in the liner of that large purse of hers. Another birth certificate. She showed it to them. She recounted how she took it to the neighboring social security office for her card, then to Barbara's Uncle Nelson, who had the tag agency, and he issued a license with that name.

"I'll never forget how the young clerk made the comment that at age eighteen, I was lucky that I never had to work, so I hadn't needed a social security card until that time! How little she knew. I kept quiet, of course. Always, the least said, the better! Perhaps some people would hear all this and say that I've lived a life of lies, but it's been a perfect life with lots of loved ones and true friends in it. There was Gail, Brian, and you, Kelly, and all the others. Then just a mere twenty years ago, there was Remington, just sitting there waiting for me! Of course, Clay, the love of my life, which I would not have found again if you, Kelly, and Brian had not wanted to marry at city hall in Wichita. And I thought at the time what a weird place to be married! But I have no regrets. And you're right, Kelly, about this birth certificate."

She took the paper that showed her as Misee Sue Stone and tore it into many small pieces as the other three looked on. She handed the pieces to Remington, who took them. "Will you dispose of these for me, dear?" she asked.

"Of course," he answered. He would do anything for her. He always had and always would.

"May I ask one more question?" Kelly asked.

Beth looked as if she were getting tired. Recalling

old memories could do that to a person, especially at her age. "Of course, what is it?" she asked.

"What is The Wilson Bush and how did it come to be in the middle of center field of the ball field?"

Chapter 54

Beth looked at C.J. "Which one of us wants to tell about that?"

"I will," C.J. said. He knew it had too many bad memories for her. "Back at the turn of the century, and that's the twentieth century, around 1900, a man named Edgar Wilson owned most of the land on that side of Cedarville. He was one of the founding fathers of the city. Anyway, there was a large mansion where the current, I guess, bleachers are now, or at least where the bleachers were when this ball game took place. The mansion wasn't maintained, for whatever reason, and it started falling down after the original family passed away. But, in his will, Mr. Wilson left all that land to the town for the specific purpose of building a ball field and bleachers, complete with lights and the works.

"In his honor, they left a large, even then, bush in center field. There never seemed any rhyme or reason for leaving it here, but the Better Yard and Garden Society of Cedarville took over the care of it, put up a plague beside it in Mr. Wilson's memory, made it their special project, and woe be to anyone who wanted to cut it down. For some reason, ball teams from other cities were willing to sign an agreement about that stupid bush, which was amazing. But we all rejoiced when it was no longer there. Oh, by the way, Misee Sue, did Kia ever say who cut that bush down?"

He looked at Beth.

She just shrugged, shaking her head. She had her suspicions that Kia might have had something to do with it, but she never asked, and, certainly, Kia would never say.

No one, through the years, knew who cut it down. Every once in a while, some of the old folk brought it up and it was discussed, but talk of it was dying out. The latest generation of ball players really knew nothing about it.

The friends were all quiet, thinking about what they had heard, each processing the info in different ways.

Beth gave a big sigh, one that made her shoulders raise and lower.

She put both hands under the newspaper article and picked it up. She looked down at it.

The moment seemed suspended in time.

Unbidden, a large teardrop formed in the corner of her right eye. With the angle of her head, it fell off her cheek and fell onto the newspaper.

It landed squarely on top of the inset of The Wilson Bush.

End

About the Author

Mary Jane Bryan is a graduate of Missouri State University (SEMO), Cape Girardeau, Missouri, with a B.S. in Business Administration/General Management and a graduate of Three Rivers Community College, Poplar Bluff, Missouri, with an AA in General Studies.

Bryan is strong believer in women as entrepreneurs and managers, and a past creator and owner of Jane's Muppets. She is past member of Toastmasters International, which is an excellent resource for creative writing and presentation, receiving critiques and advice as needed. A past resident of Ecuador, Bryan now currently resides in Farmington, Missouri, with her husband, Peter, and their cat, Cookie.

9 781644 370056